Past Praise for Gladys Swan

"Swan keeps the men and women in [ ] [ ]tersweet stories dreaming and reachin[ ] [ ]ions of American storytelling."

"Swan claims the reader[ ] [ ]gorous renderings of human experience."
—*Publishers Weekly*

"Swan creates people who touch us; she's a compassionate classicist."
—*Chicago Tribune*

"In these times of so much 'throwaway' fiction, Swan's collection shines with the timeless luster that comes from well-polished prose and a true ken for storytelling."
—*Kansas City Star*

"Her stories are rich, and, like a Chekhov or a Flannery O'Connor, she needs to be appreciated for the short works at which she excels."
—*Southern Humanities Review*

"Swan combines shared features of history and fiction. For what else is history in the final analysis than an imagining of connections? And this aspect of the stories makes them not just isolated accounts of imagined lives but metaphors for the history of our time."
—*American Book Review*

"…an enchantment worth the price of admission."
—*New York Times*

A Garden amid Fires

Also by Gladys Swan

a **Garden** amid **Fires**

stories

Gladys Swan

BkMk Press
Universitiy of Missouri-Kansas City

BkMk Press
University of Missouri-Kansas City
5101 Rockhill Road
Kansas City, Missouri 64110
(816) 235-2558 (voice)
(816) 235-2611 (fax)
www.umkc.edu/bkmk

MAC
MISSOURI ARTS COUNCIL

Financial assistance for this project has been provided by
the Missouri Arts Council, a state agency.

Cover art: "Patio with Flowers" by Gladys Swan
Cover and interior book design: Susan L. Schurman
Managing Editor: Ben Furnish

BkMk Press wishes to thank Bill Beeson, Teresa Collins, Matthew
Merryman, Andrés Rodríguez. Special thanks to Karen I. Johnson.

Library of Congress Cataloging-in-Publication Data

Swan, Gladys, 1934-
   A garden amid fires / Gladys Swan.
      p. cm.
Summary: "A collection of ten contemporary short stoires whose
characters include a Southwestern rancher's son, an Amercian
expatriate widow in Europe, a divorced New England grandmother,
and others, all of whom reach important psychological insights
through their stories' varied conflicts"—Provided by publisher.
   ISBN-13: 978-1-886157-58-3 (pbk. : alk. paper)
   ISBN-10: 1-886157-58-8 (pbk. : alk. paper)
   I. Title.

PS3569.W247G37 2007
813'.54—dc22
                    2006034004

For Richard

Acknowledgments

Greatful acknowledgment is made to the editors of the periodicals in which these stories have appeared:

Sewanee Review
Green Mountains Review
New Letters
Shenandoah
Manōa

aGarden amid Fires

On the Island

For more than a month before she actually showed up, the news was circulating that Trudie Blazer was coming back to the island. At first, I didn't give any credit to the rumor—I'd heard it before. She'd been expected any number of times, but except for a couple of brief visits during the early years of her first marriage, she never came. After that, an assortment of friends and connections and various renters kept turning up, dropping in at the marina and arranging with me for the boat to take them over. They offered the chance for a lot of comment and gossip and all kind of speculation from those of us who lived on the lake. There were some prizes, believe me. One I remember in particular, a fella who managed to alienate just about everybody before he was done, he was so sure we were there solely for his personal benefit—on hand to do his bidding and be grateful for the opportunity. He owned a small company that manufactured antiperspirants and insect repellent, which he claimed were the best on the market. He'd do us the favor of letting us buy his products. When his sailboat capsized, after he'd let it be known he was a master sailor, we were downright gleeful. We yelled a few compliments. He pulled out the next day.

Later on, Trudie's college-age kids showed up, Ned and Cindy, the older ones, then Macey and Brad, a hoard of friends in tow. I knew them a little, did various jobs and errands for them. I tried to find traces of their mother in them. In Macey I could hear her voice, though in the daughter it was shrill and grating, and the way she moved her hands somewhat reminded me of Trudie. But it seemed like she'd tried imitating her ma and overshot the mark. Brad had her hair color—golden. Handsome son of a gun—and he knew it—the way he looked out under half-lidded eyes—like a lizard sunning on a rock. Water-skied all the time he was up there, or went off to Portland for tennis meets. The girls were drawn to him like flies to honey, wouldn't you know it. The others were friendly enough, the younger girl almost as pretty as Trudie—with her freckles. I'd ask them about Trudie now and again, casual-like. She was living in Spain, they told me—then, with her second husband out in California. He had interests in Asia.

Everybody else who'd known Trudie talked about her too. The hearsay was piled so thick, it would've took a hunting knife to cut through it. By the time the younger kids were coming along, she was onto her third husband, the first having shot himself after she'd gone through his fortune—that's what was in the air—and the second one run off with another woman— to the Azores or someplace hard to locate on the map.

Occasionally her guests, especially the women who'd seen her recently, would bring each other up-to-date. I remember eavesdropping on one such conversation, among two slick-looking young women in black pants and tank tops, one redhead, the other blonde. They had some anecdote about Trudie moving one of them big hot tubs from one side of the yard to the other just because it didn't look right where it was.

"Trudie always gets what she wants," the blonde said. The redhead agreed.

I thought she might be right. When it became clear Trudie was really coming, that I'd actually see her, I couldn't help thinking about her, about the island. Not that I hadn't, but in the interests of peace and reason, I'd tried to push her out of my mind. Often enough, some image of her or a snatch of conversation would take over my brain like one of those tunes you can't get rid of, and it would sink me in a low spot. I had to look at that island every day, in all seasons and weathers, and sometimes I hated that it was there, like she was the one who'd stuck it right in front of my eyes. I had to let it bleach into being just a piece of landscape, like a tree you pass every day, but don't bother to look at. That way I could get on with it.

Her family had owned it for three generations, an island out in the middle of a lake up there in the Maine woods. Trudie's father had bought it cheap—the paper company practically gave it away. But long before that, Trudie's grandfather built a big log camp on it, pretty fancy inside. Before the days of electricity, they'd be there all summer, up till Labor Day. They even came up during the War, when everybody else was off working in the potato fields.

My dad usually closed camp for Trudie's folks, and he'd let me help. As a boy, I'd walked all through the house, a trespasser, admiring the antique desks and marble-top bureaus, sleek tables all polished, and the great granite fireplace in the living room with the deer head above it. Somehow they'd managed a baby grand, hauling it by truck over the ice, and every once in a while you'd catch some tune that found its way across the water. One summer it was Scott Joplin—I used to pause and listen, the tunes haunted me. For days afterward, they went round in my head. The house, tucked back in the pines, was a place apart like a piece of history, beyond any value you could put on it, not like ours with its auction furniture that the cats clawed and the dogs and kids flopped down on.

The island was on a different plane altogether. It was a place where people came for the sole purpose of enjoying themselves—waterskiing, skinny dipping, lying around in hammocks, drinking gin and tonics and letting the hours go by. But that wasn't but the half of it. Other things sailed beyond what you think of as pleasure, toward those hidden places where your heart's desire knocks up against the forbidden. Trudie's parents and their best friends had discovered early on they fancied each other's mates. Most folks would have swallowed up the inclination. But they had ended up swapping partners, all four of them even remarrying in the same ceremony. The two mothers kept their babies, just switching fathers before the little ones could figure out the difference. (That would have been Trudie's older brother, who died young. Trudie came from the new pairing.) When I first heard of it, I was caught in a spin of amazement: they'd just reached out and grabbed what they wanted, let people think what they pleased.

Another time, I was struck by the story that Trudie had taken her mother's diamond ring to wear and lost it when she went swimming. I was astonished that such a thing could happen, that anyone would leave a diamond ring lying around to be lost so carelessly. My mother used to rinse out plastic garbage bags so she could use them again, and my dad saved everything, straightening bent nails and keeping panes of used glass with the corners broken off, in case he could cut them down to replace some smaller pane. And when the payments were made on time that allowed us to keep the store with the narrow café on the side, the gas pump in front—home, our quarters being upstairs—there was a general sigh of relief. It was a close call sometimes. If push came to shove, there was the lot next to it with the boathouse, where we stored boats over the winter. It could have been sold, but if that money wasn't coming in, what would provide the margin next time? What we made over the summer wasn't enough to tide us over the winter, even with the storage fees. My dad guided hunters and hunted deer and partridge himself to keep us in meat, and trapped beaver to sell the skins. Every bit helped. Later on, I joined him.

When I was thirteen or fourteen—that was right after the end of World War II—and had a free moment from the chores, I'd take a canoe out and paddle around the island, careful to stay out of the way of the water-skiers skimming past, and pretending not to notice the swimmers sunning themselves on the rock at one end or diving from it into the lake. Their shouts and laughter echoed across the water.

Trudie came into the store now and then with her mother for groceries or gas, a girl about my age. She may have been small and wiry, but when I began to notice her, she had a kind of restless energy and intensity that made you want to step out of the way. She wasn't pretty, not then, but that didn't matter. It was her personality that grabbed your attention. Once she got something into her head, it was hard to shake it loose, and later when I knew her better, I wondered where the path she struck would take her. A long way, I found out.

At some point I must have thought anything she wanted must be worth more than other people's desires. I remember her throwing a fit in the store once because her mother wouldn't let her swim over to the island without someone accompanying her—she was positive she could do it. She stood there, a raging brat, freckle-faced, snub-nosed, her hair falling in her eyes, tears streaking down her face, red with rage and frustration. Perhaps then—why, I still can't explain—I knew I loved her.

A few years later I'd be spending a lot of time on the island. I'd always been handy with tools. I grew up with them, as well as guns and fishing gear, working alongside my dad, first handing him things, then learning how to use them—fixing whatever needed fixing: leveling the foundations of old camps, working on motors, building docks, painting boats, cutting trees. A couple of summers I went down to the coast for a couple of weeks to help my uncle out in his boatyard, and he taught me carpentry.

The summer I was seventeen—that must have been the summer of '48—my dad and I went over to the island to take down a tree that had been struck by lightning and was a threat to the house. Dad handed up the chain saw, the first we owned, after I shinnied up the tree, and I took off a bunch of the limbs. Then my dad took her down, and we sawed up the trunk and bigger branches, and piled up the wood for the fireplace. While we were at it, Mrs. Blazer was right there on hand and some of their guests stood on the porch watching. She was full of admiration. "You've done a splendid job—just splendid, the way you landed that tree." If she said so, it had to be true, she had such a thrilling voice. It went through you, played a few cords along your spine, raised the level of your blood and left its vibration in the air. It made you forget who you were and what you were doing and called you in the direction of some special moment.

I stood there wiping the sweat off my forehead and neck with one of them big red kerchiefs I'd brought along—also good for keeping the black flies off your neck. She handed my dad some money and said, "How about something, a beer or a lemonade. And you are staying for lunch, aren't you?"

She was like that—my dad not only worked for her over the years, he'd listened to her troubles—her husband had been killed in a hunting accident—and she would ask his advice about boats and fishing and termites and anything else that was on her mind.

"I would appreciate a glass of water," my dad said. "Then I've got to get back to the store."

She asked Trudie to bring it. "Can't I give you some lunch?" she said. "Coral has it just about ready."

My dad thanked her, but he wouldn't stay—he had a dozen things waiting for him back at the marina.

"Maybe Arthur could stay," Mrs. Blazer suggested.

Perhaps he caught the stir of my desire—what her voice had called up— because he said, "Sure, if you want to. Only I've got to get back."

"We'll bring him over," Mrs. Blazer said.

It was like I'd been let out of a pen and admitted to a greener pasture—my mom had never gone over to the island herself, and my dad and I mainly for work we had to do. But there I was, at the long table off the kitchen like I was one of the company, with Coral's chicken pie and fresh peas in front of me, and generous slices of her home-made bread—while Trudie and her friends talked about clothes and movie stars and films they wanted to see and wasn't it a rum town that didn't get anything but what they'd already seen. They were always driving the ten miles it took them to get to "civilization," as they called it. Only the way they said it, you knew they meant it was nothing but a paper-mill town out in the middle of nowhere. If you wanted anything special, you had to order it or drive all the way to Bangor.

Then they shifted to local stuff so as to include me. The lake wasn't the greatest for fish, they were saying, though it had been good for white perch before they stocked it with bass. Todd had caught a bass early that morning. Most of the time I didn't go out—I had too much to do around the store. The two boys, Todd and Max, and their sister lived down on the coast above Portland, and they went out in the bay with their dad and various uncles. The men sometimes came up in the fall to go hunting. Todd had gone out with his cousin that fall, wounded a buck. They'd tried to track it through the woods, but lost it. Maybe this year they'd hire my dad and me for guides.

The woods and lake were in my blood, ever since childhood. I knew things I couldn't even put in words. But somehow I always tried to imagine life in other places, life of a different character. Maybe that's what books did to me—putting myself into other people's lives. Mrs. Nash, the school librarian, used to suggest books for me to read. Seems like most of the people I read about threw away their chances and never got what they wanted. There was this thing that kept pulling at them, wouldn't leave them alone, and the ones I read about just moiled around and never seemed to get it right. They made me feel dismal, yet, except for Trudie, they seemed more real than most of the people I knew.

All I know is that island became what I dreamed over, and Trudie Blazer was somehow the one who stood for what I wanted. A powerful discontent rose up in me, as though there ought to be something more, something better than the woods and this lake, because other people lived elsewhere and did things that caught my imagination. I knew too many guys over the years that couldn't get above their guns, their trucks, their fishing gear, and their dicks. And when the light hit the island just around sunset, pouring gold all over the trees, I just knew there had to be more.

"Arthur," my mother would say sharply, when I got restless and down in the mouth, "where is your head? You're not going to turn into some kind of dreamer—I won't have it. Too many things around here need doing. You moon around like that and I'll get out the tonic." Then I'd have to snap to.

17

But they of the island were different—they had their tennis lessons and their parties and went off to private schools. They'd been cut out for different lives. I wanted some of it. Especially since I was stuck where I was—my folks barely had enough to get by on, let alone money for me to go off even to college. They couldn't spare me. I would spend my life helping run the store or café, fixing this and building that, oiling guns and taking a knife to fresh kill. I even liked doing those things; yet there was something, call it style, about the way Trudie and her friends conducted themselves: the way the girls shook their hair back from their heads and operated their cutlery; the way the guys knew how to be polite and confident in the way they talked about sports or "the old man" and jostled one another, and laughed—confident that certain things belonged to them that I could never lay claim to.

I can see them now out on the float, lazing in the sun, teasing one another, the girls, lean and long legged, hair all bleached by the sun, their lovely breasts so tantalizing to the imagination. And the guys, sleek and tan, their white teeth flashing the sun. Every now and then one would take a dive into the lake and come up, breaking the surface like a porpoise. They moved through the water without effort while I stood by watching.

When I was in high school, I'd go out with a couple of my buddies to swim and dive off the rock, if nobody was on the island. Once in a while I'd go by myself to watch the sunset, trying to see what they saw, trying to imagine what it was like to see things from an island, to look out from it toward the shore.

Just as I left after lunch the day we felled the tree, Trudie came running up and punched me on the arm, so hard it hurt. "You got muscles, Arthur," she said. "You're a skinny rat, but you've got muscles. Come back so we can feed you." She laughed and ran off, and the others laughed too as I stood there bewildered.

"Oh, dear Arthur, don't mind her," Mrs. Blazer said in her thrilling voice—she could have sung opera. "That's just Trudie," as though she was some spirited animal you needn't waste your time trying to tame.

"Oh, Trudie," one of the boys teased her, and rolled his eyes.

After that, she acted as though I was just a fly on the wall, and if I tried to act friendly, she gave me a slow considering look like I was invading her territory. The next summer, though, the summer I was eighteen, Mrs. Blazer came over to see if I could do some work for her. The old camp had been neglected. There were rotting logs that needed replacing, and then when she got that done, she'd see what else needed doing.

I saw Trudie when I went over, and it seemed to me she'd metamorphosed over that year into a different creature. And maybe I was looking at her with a sharper focus, noticing her figure, the way she moved. She was rambunctious as ever, still said whatever came into her head and acted like some impulse drove her that wasn't clear even to her. She had wonderful eyes, dark and expressive, and a wide mouth. Her voice, like her mother's, thrilled me. It lingered in my head without words, beckoning me, promising what I could never name. I loved the agony.

I went over and started on the logs—four needed to be taken out and new ones set in. As soon as I was halfway into the job, Mrs. Blazer decided the windows and doors needed new screens. "There's another little thing I'd like you to do," she said, like it was nothing at all and I could just throw it in. And I found myself doing more than the job called for, putting in extra hours I didn't charge her for. Finally she wanted the camp painted as well, and when I came up with a price, she said, "Well you know, we've given you a lot of work. Couldn't you trim it down just a little?" She could have asked me for anything.

My dad was put out with me. "You don't have to give your time away," he told me. "You told her a fair price. They've got money…"

"I'm just glad to have the work," I said. "I'm getting a reputation," I insisted.

"—for being a fool," he said. "Plus you're making it hard for yourself and for the other boys trying to earn a living."

But I had my reasons. I'd been seeing Trudie all along. She was by herself for a time—her friends were coming up in

August—and when I paused for a little time-out, she'd have me come and sit down on the porch, and look at me with her splendid eyes. Whatever she said in that voice, more and more like her mother's, made me vibrate down to the toenails, so that when, like her mother, she asked me if I'd have a glass of lemonade, I felt as though I were receiving some special gift. "You're wonderful, just wonderful," Mrs. Blazer would say as she admired my work. And Trudie: "How did you learn to do all that?"

Maybe they convinced me I was something beyond a lowly handyman; instead, a prince in disguise. Otherwise how could I have gathered up my nerve and asked Trudie if she'd like to go to a movie.

"Why, that would be terrific," she said, without a pause. "I thought you'd never ask."

I had been anointed.

"You just be careful there," my mother warned, the night we were going.

"Oh, Ma," I said, "you know I wouldn't do anything."

"That's not what I mean," she said. "It's not her I'm worried about."

We had a good time. It was some silly Doris Day movie, but it could have been anything, I wouldn't have known what it was about. I kept looking away from the screen, checking to see whether she was really sitting next to me. Once she turned away from her concentration and smiled at me, and I reached over and took her hand. She didn't pull away.

Afterward we took a long walk out under the stars and exchanged regrets about the summer ending, though it was only the beginning of August.

"I don't really want to go to college," she said.

I looked at her.

"What's so great about it, except for the parties? I think I'll take French, though. I love Edith Piaf. What I'd really like to do is get on a boat and sail around the world. You know, visiting foreign countries."

"And then?"

"I don't know—maybe just keep sailing. What about you?"

"I'd like that fine if you'd take me along."

She laughed. I was afraid she'd tell me I was sweet, or something that would make me feel like a jerk; instead she reached up and kissed me. I was about to put my arms around her and go for the real thing, but she slipped away and held up her watch. "Ten o'clock. You've got to get me back to the island."

Dutifully I took her over, and Mrs. Blazer met us at the dock. We stood there laughing and talking for another quarter of an hour. When I got back, I was too excited to sleep. I was tossed among various fantasies, sexual and otherwise. Trudie and I on some other island, tropical maybe, alone together. Maybe that's what all love stories come down to, that longing to get away from where you are and what you are, to quench your burning in another's flame—to live blind and dumb except for that.

But after our one little date, it was all business, and when I went over to work, Trudie was never around—she was off with her friends, who'd finally arrived. Mrs. Blazer still came out to praise my accomplishments. Then she'd take me off to show me some broken or worn out thing she found almost too complicated to consider, and would brighten up when I told her I could fix it—no problem. And if it wasn't too expensive.... She couldn't have found anybody to do it cheaper. I worked through most of the fall and built a dock for her after the ice went out the next spring.

That summer Trudie was back from her first year of college. I'd written her a long letter, awkward and tiresome no doubt, with bits of news about people she knew and news of what I was doing, ending with the hope I'd be seeing her. I had a surprise waiting for her, I told her. I'd gotten a fellow I knew, French-Canadian down from Quebec, who had a contract to cut timber, to teach me a little parlez-vous during the winter in the exchange for overhauling his truck. I wrote down everything he told me; then I'd try for significant conversation. Trudie didn't answer, so I had to wait 'til summer to try my French out on her.

"Trudie, *ma chérie. Comment ça va?*"

She laughed. "You did that? No kidding? I gave it up after a semester. The French never really learned how to spell anything. I'm going into sociology. See you," she said, and turned to leave.

I had to give her a chance to take me out of my confusion. "What is it, Trudie? I haven't seen you for a whole year and—"

"You have some kind of claim on me?" she said. "We went to the movies for God's sake. It was something to do—"

"I just thought—"

"Listen," she said slanting her head, looking at me like an owl questioning my sanity, "what could you possibly offer me?"

I knew suddenly what I'd hidden from myself all along. "What do you want?"

She looked into my face. "Everything," she said. "I want a man to give me everything." She turned and walked away.

It took me a while to pick myself up off the ground. My fantasies had carried me into a dimension where only the island was visible and veils of colored smoke trailed over me—all obstacles had fallen away. Mrs. Blazer would take me into her husband's sporting business she still managed, teach me the ropes. Or else if that fantasy grew threadbare, another sidled in from the opposite direction: Trudie would leave all behind and we would be poor but happy together.

She was looking for a piece of property—that's what had really brought her back, as much as any sort of nostalgia. The son and daughter from the first marriage were having some kind of squabble with the son of the second marriage and the daughter of the third or maybe they were all feuding with each other. It was hard to get things sorted out: who had prior rights to the island and where it was going to end up as a piece of inheritance. They all wanted it under certain definite conditions. The debate had grown hot and rancorous. Cindy wasn't speaking to Brad, and Ned insisted he had the prior claim—only they could keep it straight. Trudie had approached the owner of the old mill just down the river a few miles away, but it was an impractical scheme, and besides the kids wanted a place on the lake. So Trudie explained matters to me as she let it be known she was looking for a piece of property, and did I know anybody who might be willing to sell. That way the family feud could be settled and the two younger kids could have a place of their own. She tried to make it sound like an ordinary matter, but her hand kept clenching and unclenching the car keys she was holding.

I told her I'd keep a lookout but that nothing offered at the moment. The lake had been building up over the years, properties were scarce, and people were anxious to keep what they got. My place was worth some money if I'd wanted to sell it.

I hadn't recognized her when she first came in. The years hadn't been exactly kind, but then she was pushing seventy pretty hard. Her complexion was mottled, her face deeply lined, and her hennaed hair, though elegantly styled, didn't succeed in making her look young. I will say her eyes still drew me—dark and intense—and her voice could still make the air tremble.

"You've really made something of this place," she said looking around.

I acknowledged the compliment—I'd completely rebuilt it. "Yes, Margaret and I worked hard." Perhaps she knew I'd married, perhaps not.

"Children?"

"Afraid not. We lost one, couldn't have any more."

She acknowledged this with a sigh. "You know I think of those summers back on the island—we were happy then, weren't we?"

"I suppose," I said, with a shrug. "And did you find him?" I asked her.

"Find who?"

"The man who'd give you everything?"

She leaned back and roared with laughter. "Oh," she said, in the voice I could recall so well, "you knock me out, you really do. Arthur," she said, "you know what I'd like—I'd like to give you a hug, a great big hug."

23

I waited to see what made me specially deserving.

"Oh, don't be put off," she said. "I'm just blundering on." She looked at me for a moment as though considering. A look that was almost tender. "What do you think it would be like if we took up where we left off—"

"Rewrite the script?" I said. "What could I give you now that you'd want?" But I knew—it was the piece of land I owned, a piece of inheritance, because I had no one special to leave it to now that Margaret was gone.

I could see in her eyes how she wanted it or whatever that represented. At first I wondered why she couldn't let her kids thrash things out for themselves. But then it occurred to me she couldn't let go, not when something seized hold of her imagination. And this she had to have too—with her stamp on it to take forward into the future toward the horizon where the path ended. She might have to pass out of the picture, but something would be there, right there where she stepped off— marked with her intensity. She stood up suddenly. "I have to be going," she said. "Brad's coming in later. Come over to the island," she said. "Please come." She reached out for my hand and gave it a squeeze.

I accompanied her down to the dock and watched her get into her boat, start up the motor and take off. It was a wonderfully clear afternoon, balmy, the edge of the mountains beyond the lake cut out sharply against the sky. Next door, a couple of men were getting ready to take off in their motor boat. Renters up from New Jersey. A tall fellow with glasses and a young guy with a bald spot. They had family visiting. Kids were out for a swim, one little girl on the dock throwing a Frisbee for a black lab that swam toward it like his life depended on it. The other kids were paddling around on rafts, splashing and yelling, having a whale of a time. Toward the shore, but out of reach of the commotion, three older women, heavyset with heavy arms, were standing in the water up to their breasts. I watched them as they stood there, sagging somewhat under the weight of their bodies, the sun on their white swimming caps, as they chatted together or floated idly in the water. I could imagine them carved out of stone, standing there forever.

I stood watching them until gradually they emerged from the water. Then, unwilling to go indoors, I watched the kids, who dived and swam and threw the Frisbee for the dog until you thought they'd all drop, until they finally brought the sun down behind the trees. The clouds above the mountains were lit up with the afterglow. Then, reluctantly, they left the water and scurried into the cabin. Brad hadn't come in yet; he'd be late for supper.

The island was becoming indistinct, the pines blurring into one another, casting a darker shadow on the water. I looked over to the rock and caught sight of a figure in white sitting there to watch the sunset. She'd had on a white blouse, I remembered. The air was getting chill, and she looked singularly alone out there on the rock. For an instant, I saw the young girl sitting there, could hear her voice as the laughter floated around her. I wondered if she could see me here on the shore. I stood until the light faded from the clouds and her outline, too, merged with the shadows. And I wondered, as I turned to go inside, if she could see me now as what she couldn't have and would never get.

Uncle Lazarus

The fog had come in on something other than little cat feet, damp and impenetrable, and Mason Chalmers insisted that Kitty Bean let him off at the other side of the bridge that led down into Prospect Landing. He could get up the hill to his house on his own. Save her a trip over the winding dirt road and having to back out of his narrow driveway. As it was, she'd be some little time making her way back to the camp she had rented. Who knew when the fog would lift? He wished he could offer her a place to spend the night, but his house was emphatically occupied.

"Afraid to be seen in my company," she teased him.

If anything, he was afraid to be seen in his own, things having broken free from their moorings, it not yet being clear where they might settle. Everything seemed tentative, up for grabs. But he was in better spirits than he had been for months, thanks to her.

He leaned over, placed his hands on her shoulders, drew her toward him, and allowed the kiss to become an occasion in itself. "I'll be up next weekend," he said.

She put a finger up to his lips. "Best to make no plans."

"No," he agreed, "it's a poor idea. But . . ."

"You'll see me when you need to," she said. "And who knows, I may go off on one of my wanderings."

The years had not taken away her liveliness, her pride or determination. Her green eyes held their depth and sparkle above the lines in her face—she was still a beauty, her red hair a halo of fire around her face. And she was as maddeningly unpredictable as ever. "But you'll come back?"

"Of course I will. Haven't I always?"

"There have been some mighty long gaps in your appearances." The thought of her going off once again left him hollow.

"We came together long ago and maybe there's something yet to be plucked from the future. It's still ripening, you know. Meanwhile you've got work to do."

Was she putting him to some sort of test?—it was quite like her.

"Do be careful, Mason—let me give you warning. That situation of yours has an ugly turn to it. Family or no, those folks are not on your side. I never did catch the scent of benevolence in Emma. Nor her kids, except for Nancy—poor thing. At least she had the sense to clear out."

"I think you've guessed it," he said. "Leaves you with a hell of a lonely feeling."

This time she leaned forward, put her arms around him and as they kissed, he was taken up more forcefully than ever into what he'd always felt for Kitty Bean. "It's been a great moment, Kitty," he said, when he'd caught his breath. "One for the annals of time. There aren't all that many..."

"Your time and my time anyway." Her lilting laugh tripped down his spine like an arpeggio. She started up the motor, and he left her, reluctantly. He turned to watch her go, with no thought of moving until the last suggestion of her truck lights had dimmed into the fog.

It wasn't all that late, only a little past sunset, but it was dark already. Light trapped by fog. *Brouillard*—he liked the word that had lingered out of his college French, perhaps for just the right occasion. He had seen fogs aplenty, but this one made him seem afloat as well, to put in a special call for clarity. The harbor was pretty well socked in, but for one thin veil trailing towards the hill, nothing to suggest, though, that the fog would lift anytime soon. He stood in its midst, trying to get his bearings.

He walked over the bridge toward the store where his sister, Emma, sold gas and night crawlers and boating supplies, soft drinks and groceries. His first thought was to walk on past—seeing her would only put a damper on his spirits. The years had settled them into a series of enforced pleasantries, a cover for a distrust he acknowledged but didn't like to dwell on. He would never have told her about Kitty or anything that mattered to him. But he was in need of a few things to tide him over—a loaf of bread, a jar of peanut butter, a can of coffee, and a little cream to put in it. He'd have a cup of coffee with her, just to delay going home. No doubt his niece and nephew had cleaned out the pantry and refrigerator by now, as they'd been in the habit of doing all that long summer. Whatever else had occurred during his absence he didn't care to speculate about.

He had no one to blame but himself. He'd been hit during a vulnerable moment, not long after Hannah died—left there in an empty house with only his cat, Samson, and Charlie to come in to help him keep the place fixed up. Charlie did his shopping and was creditable with a hammer and nails, but not much good with housekeeping. There was cat hair over all the furniture and a century of dust—or so it seemed. The house smelled of neglect. "You can't go on living like that," Emma scolded him. "The place'll go to rack and ruin. And there's your health to think about. That Charlie is about as helpful as a crutch."

Then there was the problem with the well. First he got sick from what the doctor decided was food poisoning. Nothing he had eaten, he was convinced of that. Luckily it occurred to him to have his well water tested. Full of E. coli bacteria, it turned out, after having been good pure water for thirty years. The only conceivable source was Herb Watkins' goats on the land just above him. But Herb stoutly denied his goats had anything to do with it. They'd been neighbors for a dozen years, the goats having come into the picture some months before. Mason's alternatives were a lawsuit or a new well. He chose the well, as a matter of economy. It might cost him four thousand dollars, but a lawyer's fees, the pressure on his nerves, and bad blood on his borders were not worth the price.

His sister took issue with him, though it was none of her affair. But she had raised him, and had returned to her old habit of correcting his life and issuing dire warnings. "You let him get away with that? You'll put yourself out of house and home if you don't watch out. You need someone to handle your affairs."

It was clear what she had in mind. Her daughter, Marlene, and Vernon, her son-in-law, had presented Mason with an offer to buy his house—with the proviso that he would continue to live there. Thereby keeping it in the family. Keeping alive all the memories of Marlene's visits there when she was young. They'd be on hand to help take care of the place. He wasn't entirely convinced. He could smell something of motive, and very likely Emma was behind it—trying to do something for the younger generation, getting her ducks in a row. Her older daughter had come to grief, though of exactly what kind Emma refused to reveal. Marlene and Vernon were the objects of her anxious care. If he agreed, they'd have something after he was gone: his land was getting more and more valuable all the time. Their offer, he thought, was on the skimpy side.

He knew he was going to have to make some decision about his house; sheer inertia had kept him from making a final will. He resisted any idea of selling the property and moving to an apartment; he'd lived in the house for over thirty years and was fully determined to die there. It was the outer casing of his personality, of the life he'd lived within its walls. The old farmhouse he'd bought and redone had space and character. The kitchen with its pine cabinets and tongue-and-groove pine floors, full of light. The sunporch where they'd taken their meals and watched the light dim behind the old barn. And the garden. Outside he'd planted sweet peas of varied colors, and Hannah had her roses. He thought of all the auctions he and

Hannah had gone to, looking for furniture with good wood, now pieces they'd prized over anything they could have bought new. And his study with its shelves of books, mostly history and biography, along with Shakespeare and a set of the Great Books—he'd always been a reader—his computer, and on the walls, a couple of landscapes his mother had painted with a delicate touch, a certificate from the community commending him for his volunteer work.

If he sold the house to his niece, he'd have a little extra cash. He could pay off the debts that had come with Hannah's illness and his own time in the hospital and have something left over to leave to Charlie, who'd been with him for the past fifteen years. He said he'd consider it.

Apparently that was enough to convince Marlene and Vernon to come up from Augusta that summer, ostensibly to visit and to help him get back on his feet, but it became clear they had no intention of leaving. They moved in on him and took charge, as though they owned the place already.

They were hardly in the doorway when they told Charlie he was no longer needed. No use keeping him on, simpleminded as he was, unable to follow instructions unless you repeated them three or four times and supervised his every move.

"But it's his job," Mason insisted. "He's been with me ever since he hurt his back up at the mill." He'd put his foot down, but behind his back, they made Charlie's life so miserable, Charlie had left on his own. "You'll save twelve thousand dollars a year," Emma told him sagely. He was furious, not simply that they'd taken advantage of his weakness, but that he'd slipped into a certain lack of nerve.

As he drew closer, he saw a car sitting in front of the store, with Emma outside filling up the gas tank; she stood talking to the driver as he was counting out the bills. She knew everyone for miles around and pumped her regulars for gossip as they bought groceries and parts and fishing tackle and bait. Mason's brother-in-law, Homer, a taciturn man and exacting mechanic, serviced their boats and trucks. The two of them had put away a tidy sum at one point, but had lost considerably in the stock market.

"Well, Norman, you drive careful here in this fog," Emma said. There was a little conversation between them.

"No," Emma said. "After Marlene reported him missing, they had half the state out looking for him. Well, you heard the commotion. Helicopters flying over. Dogs tracking through the woods. Homer was gone for three days dragging the bay, along with the others—left me with all the work. He's dead tired. And I'm dead tired, let me tell you. All that labor for nothing."

The driver must have sympathized. Mason drew closer.

"I'd hate to say it, but… I'm sure he took his own life." There was a catch in her voice. "Nothing to live for after Hannah passed…. Didn't leave a note or anything…. That's right—the memorial's coming up the end of the week."

He felt as though someone had landed a punch in his gut. He'd gone off without telling anybody where he was headed. Marlene and Vernon didn't have to know his every move—they weren't his keepers. It was a piece of resentment on his part. He hadn't figured they'd put him in his grave while he was gone.

He waited 'til she had a chance to put the bills in the cash drawer, glanced in to see that she was alone and stepped inside. She had sat down on a stool behind the counter and opened the newspaper, perhaps to see what they were saying about him.

When she looked up and saw him, her normally impassive face—eyes that didn't miss a trick—was fixed in something more powerful than dismay. She stood up jerkily, pressed her hand to her mouth and gave a half-suppressed cry.

"I know why you've come haunting," she said in a tight voice. "They couldn't find your body and you don't have the peace of the grave. Oh, Mason," she said, "that it should come to this." She held out a hand as though to stop his further advance. "We all understand… how sometimes you can't go on. Just tell us where the body is," she said. "and we'll bury you right and proper. And where you've put the will."

He was himself astonished, even beyond hearing the news of his own death. It was his ghost she was seeing, even as he stood there in his Red Sox cap, his blue chambray LL Bean shirt and tan slacks and Rockport walkers, vigorous and substantial, though his beard could have done with a little trimming. She was of too practical a mind—his will, eh?—he'd have thought, to let in the supernatural with the first whiff of the untoward, but she used to scare him with tales of ghosts and hauntings when he was a boy, maybe believed in them. Or else had wanted to induce the right sort of behavior on his part—he never knew. Perhaps she had planted him so securely in the other world, had so much now invested in his demise she couldn't draw back.

He could have held up his arm with its good solid flesh and type O blood and invited her to give it a pinch, but for some reason he wasn't ready to undeceive her. The fog perhaps—must have put him in the mood.

He opted for a profound silence. He could hear the hum of the fluorescent lights on the ceiling and in the refrigerators. "Death is a hard thing, Emma," he said finally in a husky whisper—"when you *haven't* run out of things to live for."

She was silent as well, having to reconstruct his fate. "What happened to you, Mason?" she said, with a hint of desperation. "We've searched everywhere."

"I went fishing, Emma."

"Fishing? Why, you haven't been fishing for over a year, not since…."

"Fortunately, I got out of the slough of despond. Ray Thompson came along.

You don't know Ray—a regular cutup when he was young. Sold me a boat once that I swear had the inclination of a horse forever pulling toward the stable. And we've drunk many a beer together. Great fisherman. I can remember a time…." Though the power of invention could have taken him by a longer route, he let it go. "He'd rented a camp up on Matawamkeag and came down after me. Hadn't seen one another in I don't know how long. Just came and collected me and took me off in his truck. 'Mason,' he said, 'let's see what we can do. This is just the lake for white perch— And you know as well as I do they're the best eating of all…'"

"You went that far?" She was putting things together. "So that's why your truck's right here—parked in front of the house.

And no note or anything, about where you'd gone. We thought …."

Yes, I know what you thought. He watched her as she made an effort to work out the perplexity of things. He tried to make a space for contrition—he hadn't meant to give anyone trouble over him, but things had gone beyond him, and he was being carried forward in the momentum. It was no longer possible to continue what he'd been experiencing lately—an odd detachment from his own life.

The only help he managed to give her was to extend the plausibility of his fiction.

"Only once I got fishing, the old appetite just came back. Ray had some business up in Houlton, so I got up early that last morning and went out on my own. I was out there in the middle of the lake when a line squall came up—a real doozey. Tried to get back before it struck, but it hit that boat and turned it around like a leaf, and the waves kicked up and suddenly I was swept out into the lake."

"Didn't you have a life jacket?"

"It got so hot before that squall came up, I took it off. Never figured anything like that would happen. Had it lying there right in front of me."

She stared at him, unblinking, but whether she'd swallowed the tale was unclear. The phone rang, and they both gave a start. When she turned away to answer it, he took the opportunity to slip away. He'd floated in the front door, so to speak, and caught her unaware, and it seemed a good moment to drift out again, disappear.

He counted on her to work things out afterward, figure he'd been playing her like a fish. Right now she was too rattled to think straight. Moments later he could hear her calling after him, but the fog was against her. For good measure, he ducked into the trees and stood there, fueling another emphatic silence. *I am a figment of my own imagination,* he thought.

"So tell me about your life," Kitty Bean said to him. They'd taken the motorboat out on the lake over to a spot near the far

shore that, Kitty said, was promising for white perch. It was warm
and sunny, a fine day in August, moving toward September.
You could tell that things were winding down, the leaves of
the trees having grown rusty, as though they'd done their duty
for the year. A few branches of the maples were going red in
the swamps. But the goldenrod, all different species with their
various heads and shapes, and the other late-summer flowers—
asters and sunflowers were still offering their vigor. And he had
cause for celebration because Kitty Bean had come back once
more, come for him, and they were sitting together there on
the water, with a picnic basket of food she'd put together, thick
meat sandwiches, and potato salad, dill pickles, chocolate chip
cookies, and a thermos of lemonade.

He was back in another place and time—past his domestic
troubles, past all thought of politics and war and the drift of
the country, past the need to sort through the fictions that
daily confronted him in the newspapers and on television and
brought him to anger and cynicism. Small comfort that Hamlet
had had a similar problem. But now there were just the two of
them sitting there with most of their lives behind them, but
still holding the vital thread of what had brought them together
after all their separations. She had come for him, just come out
of the morning in her truck and said, "Mason, here I am—I've
come to spirit you away." And what could be better, out there
on the lake with a fishing pole in his hand and Kitty sitting
across from him.

He could reach all the way back to origins: *Kitty Bean, Kitty
Bean.* His cousin's name had reverberated in his head with the
rhythm of promise and delight, like a sky full of colored balloons.
In kindergarten, he'd spun himself around with the rhythm of
her name, and she, too, had spun around and around, the two of
them breathless and giddy out there on the playground. Until,
at the center of the whirling, a flame shot up and engulfed him,
heart and senses, liver and lights. He'd turned about in that
flame through all his childhood and youth, even when her face
had grown beyond his remembrance of her. Through the years
that turned it was the flame of his longing.

His first experience of loss came when he was six and his aunt and uncle moved off to New Mexico, taking Kitty with them. "Kitty's your cousin," his mother said. "You'll have to find another girlfriend." But then there was the tentative rediscovery of one another the summer his aunt and uncle came back East for an extended visit. The two of them were inseparable, hunting frogs together and fishing off the end of the dock. He'd given her his pocketknife, he reminded her. "Still have it," she told him.

"Then when I came out to New Mexico that summer to help your folks with the orchard, they treated me like a member of the family." A feeling he'd never had with his father, or Emma, seven years older than he, who took over the household when his mother died. His aunt made his bed and washed his clothes and plied him with food and his uncle taught him to ride a horse and let him drive his truck.

"Well, you were."

"The thing I chiefly remember," he said, "when I had the words to tell myself was that suddenly I knew what love was. It was a discovery. My head was all full of you, but it was in the air, and I'd got hold of some of it—people treating one another not just like they mattered, but as though they could *see* you, see who you were and actually loved *that*. Maybe I'd never have known how it could be done…"

She smiled. "My mother said she thought you were love-starved and undernourished as well. 'That tightfisted brother of mine—I never could find much sugar in the bucket.'—that's what she said."

He laughed. "Maybe that's why she kept trying to feed me."

When they sat down to breakfast, the food was spread before him like a feast. Eggs and pancakes, bacon and sweet rolls. Though it was Kitty he wanted to look at, his Aunt Mary also took his notice as he watched the way she prepared a meal, the way she handled every vegetable and piece of fruit—as though a single lettuce leaf was something to be prized. And the way they were all gathered around the table, his uncle Clyde and the three girls and his aunt. The smells that lingered in the air, a distillation.

"It wasn't just food," he said, taking up one of Kitty's sandwiches. "It was what you put into it, the feeling when you sat down to eat it. More than what you put in the stomach..." It was moments such as these—ports of entry, he liked to think of them—where you entered a certain space that belonged forever to your imagination. Among all the seething possibilities of things coming together and falling apart, you had a sudden hope of clarity about what mattered. And whatever happiness he'd had in his life, it was owing to those moments that he carried with him that served as a kind of paradigm for what he tried to create for himself.

"Too bad we didn't get married," he said to her.

"With two families beating on us about the idiot children we'd produce," she said. "There'd have been hell to pay."

He'd written Kitty love letters all the time he was in the army, but he'd never gotten any response. Kitty told him later that she'd never received the letters.

"We didn't have to have children," he said.

He had a bite on his line and tried to set the hook. "Got away," he said. He baited the hook again.

She shrugged. "I didn't think about that at the time. As it was, all I could do was go my own way, beat my head against stone walls. Not that I got all that far—probably we'd have ruined one another. You had a good long marriage, a place in the community," she offered. "Nothing to sneer at. I've been a rolling stone."

Indeed he'd loved his wife, though he'd have said now there was something left over that he'd never found a place for except in his imagination. Ironically, they'd been childless. Meanwhile Kitty had had five husbands, owing to, he thought, no one being able to meet her match. Very likely she'd have been too much woman for him as well. Most likely she'd come into the world with a certain elevation of spirit, and hadn't settled for anything less.

"When you married that first time, I was wild with jealousy." What was jealousy but the flame turned green?

"Gus?" she said. "I gave him a hard time. He probably had reason to be jealous of you."

And what would he find now when he came back home, hardly his own anymore? Not simply occupied—usurped. Very likely Marlene would be working on the afghan she was copying out of some women's magazine. And Vernon would be planted in front of the TV, where he spent most of his time when he wasn't writing the Westerns that were going to make him rich, if not famous. He'd never been West, though he read Westerns by the dozen and took his landscapes from the pictures he saw in *The Arizona Highways* he thumbed through in the library. Nor did he know anything of the habits of horses or cattle, or, Mason concluded, of men and women.

Meanwhile he palmed off his badly typed efforts to anyone who'd read them—maintaining they were at least as good as anything on the shelf in the Rite-Aide. Mason had been a captive audience. These were narratives filled with lawlessness and violence—holdups, cattlerustling, train robberies, shootings, hangings and general mayhem. "You might throw in a little sex," Mason suggested at one point, "just for the sake of variety. It's what people like to read about." Vernon worried over the subject for a while, then whipped a sheet out of the typewriter to show him. Mason was struck that he'd managed to do the job in a single sentence: *And then Nat Darby entered the saloon, took one of the girls upstairs and had his way with her. "I needed that," he said.*

During these labors, there were nearly three hundred pounds of him to keep stoked up. Mason did the cooking. That summer with Kitty had permanently influenced his ideas about food. During those years she was in charge, Emma had been able to put food on the table, mostly things she got out of a can. She could fry an egg and do up potatoes and macaroni and cheese, and she passed that knowledge on to him when she ran off to marry Homer. His father was gone most of the time, as captain of a ferryboat that went over to Saint John, and Mason fended for himself. Sometimes when he was home, they went out to eat. His father would go into the restaurant, leaving him to wait outside in the car. When he'd finished his meal, he'd bring Mason a hamburger. Once, bored with waiting, he got out of the car and went up to the window to look inside. His father was sitting practically next to the window, a plate in front of him with a steak and potatoes and all the trimmings. He ducked down quickly.

Once he learned what food could be, he decided to learn how to cook and had his aunt Mary show him all her recipes. He carried home this new knowledge, and during the time he was in college on a scholarship, he earned his spending money weekends as the cook in a small café. After his marriage, he did his share of the cooking.

Usually he started the day with baking biscuits for breakfast, and at least twice a week, he baked bread. Much better than the store stuff. He made pound cake and oatmeal cookies and yeast rolls. He gave much of it up for church bazaars or sent it round to the neighbors. Friends he invited over for roast chicken and dressing and mashed potatoes and gravy and vegetables that weren't cooked to death. And his homemade strawberry ice cream was cause for celebration. His niece and nephew tucked in three square meals without the blink of an eye; at least Marlene helped him afterwards with the dishes. But the way the two of them packed it away, going through his meatloaves and mashed potatoes, loaves of bread and plates of cookies, all the groceries and ingredients out of his own pocket—the way they sponged off him, had turned him cranky and sullen.

When he suggested to Vernon that they chip something in for all they'd consumed that summer, his niece was not pleased. Finally, after waiting a week, they handed him fifty dollars.

He walked along trying to imagine how he would arrange his appearance. If the TV was on, he could enter without their hearing him, just appear out of nowhere. Would they, too, take him for a ghost come back to his old haunts? Full of portent, and not exactly friendly. By now Emma had very likely phoned them up. Would she have raised the question of how he'd managed to keep hold of that baseball cap in the middle of a squall? "I was sure it was his ghost—like to scared me half to death. Only now I'm wondering. But if he's not dead... but can he really be alive?"

More than likely, Samson would settle the argument. Mason was sure he'd jump down from where he'd been curled up in his favorite chair, or else come out from under it to rub up against his leg—a dead giveaway. The cat had missed him terribly when he'd been in the hospital, had been all over him when he came home. Since Vernon and Marlene's arrival he'd spent a good deal of time hiding under Mason's favorite armchair. They didn't like the cat. "Now what's going on here," he could hear Vernon saying. "Folks all stirred up thinking you're dead. Maybe you can fool my mother...."

He would spare them further ambiguity. He was now ready to emerge—solid, reanimated—out of the fog. "It's your Uncle Lazarus," he'd announce to them, "—come back from the dead." And when they'd taken that in— "I have a message for you—you can pack up your stuff and clear out. Tonight you can spend with your mama. And come for the rest of your things tomorrow. Charlie'll be here to help you." The idea had just struck him.

Charlie—of course, Charlie. Back as before, as he deserved to be—rescued from betrayal. If he would come back....

That meant that he had one more place to visit before he set foot in the house. It would take him an hour—more with the fog—to get to Charlie's trailer, where he lived with his wife, Jenny. Whereas Charlie was slow, Jenny was quick, and together they'd made a decent life. Their two grown daughters, both married, worked part-time waitressing in a restaurant up the coast.

Mason could take a little credit for him. He'd come upon Charlie when he was a juvenile officer for the county. Charlie had run away from the foster home where he'd been placed, having been shunted from one relative to another, mostly neglected and very likely abused, and was living on the streets. What to do with him. The kid was sixteen and on the verge of getting into real trouble. Mason did what he frequently did with the kids he worked with—he took him fishing, taught him to fish. He'd found that out about some of those who came his way—if they took to fishing and enjoyed the companionship, they could get a glimpse of something beyond what they knew. He saw to it the boy got through high school—he wasn't the brightest, but he could get that far. And he was willing to work. He earned some real money working for the paper mill in Brewer, till he hurt his back. Then Mason took him on—Charlie needed work, and Mason needed somebody to help him keep the place up.

As Mason approached, Charlie's dog, a combination golden retriever and Newfoundland, made such a racket that through the window he could see Charlie get up from his arm chair, slowly because of his arthritis, and move toward the door to see about the ruckus. Mason waited for him to open it. "What's got into you, dog?" Charlie yelled out into the fog.

"Hello there, Charlie," Mason said, stepping in close, while Charlie quieted the dog. "We haven't seen each other for a while."

Stunned, Charlie stared at him for a moment, as he stood there in the fog, then came hurtling down the steps and threw his arms around him. "I knew you weren't dead, Mr. Chalmers. I told it to Jenny. I said, 'I don't care what anybody says. He'll be back.'"

A big man, Charlie, and for a moment it seemed to Mason he'd be swept off the ground, what with him and the dog leaping up.

"Well, it's a good thing I'm here—" Mason said, when they'd got their footing and he'd caught his breath. "Seeing the state I left things in. I don't need to draw you a map."

Charlie gave a little self-conscious laugh.

"Come over to the house tomorrow," Mason said, "that is, if you're willing—after all this nonsense."

Jenny, who was standing in the doorway looking over the scene, didn't wait for his response. "Of course he'll come," she said. "He's been moping around here all summer. I'll be glad to get rid of him."

"Make it about nine," Mason said. "We'll have a cup of coffee—you and me with no interference—and I'll make you a list of what needs doing."

41

"You want me to pick up some doughnuts on the way?" Charlie asked. "I mean, if you don't have anything on hand."

"I'd count it lucky if there was a sack with crumbs in it. Chocolate icing on mine." He couldn't remember when he'd last made doughnuts; maybe he'd get out the recipe one of these days.

He'd be busy for a while. He'd have to send Charlie for groceries before he could do any cooking. Meanwhile he'd throw open every window, air out the whole place. Change the sheets. Remove all trace of recent occupancy. He'd see if Mrs. Gresham would come in to do some cleaning, or one of the other church ladies. He had an accumulation in the closets and basement, stuff that had piled up over the years. No point in saving it. Some of Hannah's clothes he could give to the church for their rummage sale. And now that he was free to live, he'd make an appointment with Collins, the lawyer, to make out his will. His house would be his own, and when the time came, he'd be leaving it in good hands.

Traveling Light

Though there were brief intermittent bursts of sun as they headed through the hills of eastern Pennsylvania, clouds gathered steadily over the day, with the threat of rain, louring skies. Without the solace of each other's company, for they were traveling in separate cars. Ralph was in their daughter Helen's Ford Escort, and Phoebe was driving their Nissan Sentra. They were returning from Connecticut, where they had gone to pick up Helen's car and were heading back to Indianapolis. Phoebe had been listening to Haydn and Mozart to lighten her mood; Ralph had alternated between the news and Irish folk songs. They'd come together for lunch, chicken soup and salad at a truck stop along the interstate, their conversation mostly observations about other diners, an old habit of their life together.

"Look at that old man over there. He doesn't pause. Just keeps shoveling it in, arm going like a pump handle—doesn't look to the right or left. Like nobody else is there."

And what was his singular hunger? Phoebe wondered. Did he have a tapeworm? And could he never get fed? Like their daughter?

Now the dark heaviness above them threatened to descend full force, and Phoebe had no desire to wait for a downpour.

Blinking the headlights, their agreed-upon signal, she hoped Ralph would turn off at the next exit that promised lodging. It was already after four, and she was bone tired. By the time they got home they would have traveled nearly a week. It was a slow trip, what with patches of fog awaiting them each morning, and trucks looming out of it, coupled with their need to keep in sight of each other.

Ralph got the message and moved to the exit. They came together in front of a Best Western, and Phoebe waited while Ralph went in to register. When he came out he signaled for her to follow, and they pulled into the parking area in front of their ground floor room. "It seems like it always rains when we cross Pennsylvania," Phoebe said.

"Maybe we're just lucky that way. Look," he said, as they carried in their overnight bags. "These folks aren't put off by a little damp."

Two motorcycles had cruised up to the space in front of the room next to theirs and stopped. The travelers were well equipped with rain gear and helmets, and as both couples descended and the men parked their vehicles, they greeted each other laughing and talking. The women freed themselves from their helmets, while the men unpacked their gear for the night. One of the women shook out a mop of curly whitish-blonde hair.

"She didn't come into the world that way," Ralph said. "Why do women want to dye their perfectly good hair?"

But that wasn't what caught Phoebe's attention. "I'd like to travel like that," she asserted, as she watched them from their picture window. "Go whipping down the highway with just the necessities."

Someday, she thought, she'd like to go to Europe with just a toothbrush and a change of clothes. A friend of hers had once traveled to Central America sitting behind her boyfriend on a Harley. When they got there, they turned around and came back. The sort of fool thing you did when you were young. But both these couples were middle-aged. Paunchy men: balding, one with a trimmed beard, the other content with a mustache.

"A potential statistic for a fatal accident," Ralph said, always the realist. "Besides you'd hate it. Hard on the kidneys for one."

Of course she'd hate it. But latent in the idea was something that appealed to her.

"I like my creature comforts," he said, as if she didn't know. "And that seat in Helen's car isn't among them. I can't wait for a hot shower and a good bed."

As the rain started pelting down, the two couples dashed inside. "Not a moment too soon," Phoebe said. "Guess they're sharing a room." How well did two sets of people have to know each other before they did that? She drew the curtain and lay down on the bed and closed her eyes, while Ralph perused the *New York Times* he'd bought at the last gas station they'd stopped at. An inveterate newspaper reader, he went through the daily offering from start to finish. He needed his daily fix of cynicism, he claimed—what better fuel. It would fill an hour before they went out to eat.

By then the rain had let up. They were able to find an Italian restaurant, Luigi's, nothing fancy, where they ate for the most part in silence, too tired for speech.

"You're not eating," Ralph said, watching her pick at her food.

Phoebe pushed aside her plate of half-eaten pasta.

"Is that a comment on the food?"

Phoebe smiled. "It just gets me," she said. "Not even telling us until it's done. Yanking Emily out of school in the midst of winter, when she's just getting over scarlet fever. Without even waiting for the end of the school year. Abandoning everything and everyone. Throwing away her degree and what she thought she wanted. What is in her head?"

He reached over and took her hand. "We can't live their lives for them." He was a quiet man who seemed always to keep a distance from things, from people. At times his stance offered a certain equanimity, but not at the moment.

"And no matter what we've done...."

"We've certainly made a lot of mistakes with Helen."

"But it isn't just that," Phoebe protested. "It's almost as if she's determined that no matter what we did it would be the wrong thing."

He shrugged. "We tried."

"Ever since she was little I've watched her put obstacles in her way—do the thing most to her disadvantage."

"Maybe our notion of what her life should be doesn't fit who she is. Maybe it's in the genes."

"But she doesn't seem to know either." And how did it all translate into experience? Biology as destiny? And where did that leave anyone in the scheme of things? Somehow their daughter seemed always to be casting about in desperation, some sort of demonic impulse pushing past everything Phoebe knew or could bring to the service of love or patience or good ideas. Some sort of forward movement seemed always cruelly lost in the chaos, the dark rush of her daughter's hysteria and panic, her disillusion and despondency. Her fear.

That was a big one. Phoebe knew a few things about fear. Had felt it over her head as Helen was propelled by those urges that kept getting her nowhere.

"I have the terrible feeling that this time—" She broke off. She didn't want to create a reality from what she feared.

"Come," he said. "It's a hard trip, and the sooner we're home, the better it'll be."

They got up and she waited while he paid the check.

At their room they entered a different climate. Loud music pulsed through the wall that separated them, with occasional bursts of raucous laughter.

"A little party," Ralph said dryly, "to celebrate our arrival."

"Do they think they're kids?" Phoebe said. She tried to concentrate on the front page of the newspaper while Ralph took a shower. She could see their neighbors flaked out on their beds with their beers and snacks, absorbed in having a good time. By now the voices sounded as though they had multiplied by three.

"Well, I know it's early, but I'm calling it a night," Ralph said, emerging with a towel around him. He put on his pajamas, then came over to where she was sitting and kissed her goodnight. "I can't sleep yet," she said. "I'll read a while."

When she looked up again, Ralph had a light snore going. The man could sleep through an air raid. But she was wide awake. She couldn't read anymore, and putting the newspaper aside, the obsessions she traveled with took over. Perhaps Ralph was right—when she stood back she saw how uselessly her mind kept making its round, over and over the same ground, without anything to show for it.

Phoebe had a sudden image of Helen at the swimming pool when she was six, running and leaping without thought into the deep end. She didn't know how to swim. Phoebe had jumped in and pulled her out. Since then Helen's life had been a series of leaps into the deep end, with calls for rescue. Each rescue a tenuous business, always under threat, despite all the therapies, all the bouts in the hospital and the countless hours devoted to her particular form of suffering. From the beginning she'd never quite fit into the world—was miserable in school, afterward in whatever job she managed to get. Brilliant, full of dreams. Hard on herself; hard on others. Then picking up to go to the next new place that promised the answer to whatever dream lived in her head—the new paradise. Europe again this time. Leaving others to pick up the pieces, as though, Phoebe thought resentfully, they were called upon to put aside any dream of their own either to foster hers or pick up the shattered remains. As though she alone were entitled to step out of the human condition.

"I don't think she believes we love her," Phoebe had said once. Now she wondered if Helen had ever loved herself. "I think she believes she's unloved by the universe." She undressed and slid into the other double so as not to disturb Ralph and lay there listening to the sounds of jubilee next door. It was past ten o'clock. Why couldn't they show a little respect for their fellow travelers? Finally, after tossing from one side to the other, she got up, put on her clothes and went to rap on her neighbors' door.

The woman with the blonde hair opened up, looked at her, and greeted her like a long-awaited guest. "Come on in," she said. "Join the party." She held out her hand. "I'm Lucile," she said. "My friends call me Lucie. And my pals call me Lu. That's after the initiation," she added with a laugh.

"Look, Lucile," Phoebe said, "I'm dog tired and—"

"You look a bit worn around the edges," she said, giving

her a straight look. "I know the feeling. Give yourself a little boost and have a drink with us. A nightcap," she persisted, with such good humor Phoebe was disarmed. Too much for her this well-stacked, broad-hipped woman poured into her blue jeans, formidable in her dark blue Western shirt and looped silver earrings, her eyes accented with shadow and liner, her lips quite perfect. "You're next door, aren't you? And we're keeping you up. I'm sorry—no hard feelings, okay? We'll be knocking it off at eleven—pronto. C'mon, have a drink. You look like you need one."

"Have a drink with us," the other voices chorused. "We're celebrating." Two other couples she hadn't seen before were sitting around on the beds and chairs. They introduced themselves—Jerry, a chunk of a man with bushy black hair and beard—Mack, thin, with a narrow-shouldered scholarly look; their wives, Karen and Marcella, the first a mere child compared to the others. A cradle robbery, Phoebe thought.

Her glance took in one after the other. Look, she wanted to say. You don't know me. I don't like motor cycles. Not really. I hate TV and video games and loud music, and telemarketers, and cell phones, and I don't go to church. Right now I'm bone-tired and…. "Well, just one," Phoebe said and then thought, I didn't say that. Someone else had spoken from inside her skin. When had she ever barged into strange company?

"You just come right in, hon," Lucie said.

"We've got beer and Jack Daniels," said one of the hosts, beer in hand. "Greg," he said, shifting it so that he could shake hands with her. "Don't mind us. We're harmless."

"A little Jack Daniels," she said, resigned. She wasn't one to go stalking off to the management to complain.

He handed her a plastic cup and the bottle. "There's ice, if you want it, water in the pitcher."

"Come over here," Lucie said, after she'd introduced everybody. "Tell us where you've come from and where you're going. Tell us your story. Here, make way, you guys. What's your name, darlin'?"

"Phoebe?"

"Well isn't that special? A little room here? You can move

over, Patsy. She's my sister. Half-sister to be exact, but we're sisters all the way to the bottom."

They didn't look much alike. Patsy was small and short, a pert-looking woman, with pushed up nose and bright eyes. Her hair was hennaed.

"Phoebe?" Patsy said, considering. "Never knew anybody named that."

"It's a bird," Phoebe said. "My folks were reaching for something different."

"We're birds too," Greg said. "Birds of a feather—right, Lu?"

"Just flock down that highway," Lucie said. "Every chance we got."

"Throw a couple of things in the bag and we just take off," Greg added. "That Harley'll take you anywhere you want to go."

What sort of birds, Phoebe wondered. Lonesome doves, bar birds, raucous crows, garrulous geese, night hawks?

They arranged themselves on one of the beds, and Phoebe told them they'd gone East to bring back her daughter's car to keep while she was in Europe working—if, she did not add, she could find a job or keep one once she got it.

"They do move around," Lucie said, with a sigh. "Hard keeping track of them."

"Well, mine's got a boyfriend now," Patsy said. "And he's nearly as crazy as she is."

"If he doesn't do drugs," Lucie said, meaningfully, "she's ahead of the game."

"Only, listen to this," Patsy said to Phoebe—apparently Lucie already knew the details—"now she's complaining her 'ex' is some kind of pervert—comes naked into their son's bedroom."

"I can't really believe this," Lucie said, also to Phoebe. "I think she's making it up."

Already, Phoebe thought, they were beyond any formalities. Nowadays it seemed people didn't hover over their secrets, but were ready to open their lives even before millions of people. She could have been watching a TV show. Maybe a life was just too hard to take on; yet there you were—stuck with it. May as well let everybody in on it.

"It drives me wild," Patsy said. "Why would she send Timmy there weekends if it was true? Only, leave it to her— She says, 'I've got to have some time to myself.' Is that a reason? Would she really do that if she wasn't crazy?"

"Unless she just wants to ruin Don's reputation—since he's trying to get custody. It just came to me. What do you think?" Lucie said, turning abruptly to Phoebe. "Maybe we should get an outside opinion?"

Open a door and there was a riddle being handed to her. "That's a tough one," she said, taking refuge in the whiskey. Canny or crazy or irresponsible—take your pick. And who was telling the truth? "Have you asked the boy?"

"He's only four," Patsy said. "You can't expect him to know what's going on. I think, good grief, what if she's putting ideas in his head. She has to be making it up. But if I say anything, she'll say, 'You're just against me—you've always been against me.' So I keep my mouth shut."

Lucie shrugged. "What can you do? The world gets crazier every day. Here, let me pour you a dab more."

Phoebe let her take her glass. Drink long enough with anybody and pretty soon you drank down to the common ground, where the dumpsters were and all the garbage for the common human apartment. With a kind of relief she let go of whatever kept her on the daylight track, contained, even numb. She'd better not drink too much, though—or she'd be offering them Helen, emptying the whole pot. She was afraid to know all that was in there.

"Listen," Lucie said, "People do what they want to do. And if it looks crazy from the outside—that's because we're outside. I'll bet it makes perfect sense to them."

"Something just comes over her," Patsy went on. "She tells these stories and you don't know what's true and what isn't."

"You know how little kids are," Lucie said, "how you can't tell if it really happened or they're making it up. Well, she's like that, only she's thirty-one."

Worse and worse, Phoebe thought. "Oh, that's a tough one," she said again.

"But think if she ruins his reputation," Lucie said, "he'll be out of a job, and she'll be out of child support. She's not working now. She's gained a lot of weight and she can't stand on her feet because of her arthritis. She got it young."

The whiskey tasted better and better. Phoebe hadn't had any for a long time, and it gave her a buzz. "You want to get hold of something," she said, "only it never lies flat." She patted the surface of the bed. "You try to get a fix on it, and it goes whoosh—" She flailed her arm out in front of her.

"You got it right," Patsy said. "Boy, have you got it right."

"Whoosh," Phoebe said and let her arm go again. Jack Daniels had it right. A man to make a woman happy, even two or three. It seemed as good an explanation as any.

This time one of the other men—she'd already forgotten their names—came along with the bottle. "I think you girls need another round," he said. The music had been turned down low to something sweet. At times the voices became more confidential, then erupted once again into laughter.

"I've got one for you too," Lucie said.

"Riddle me, riddle me," Phoebe said, "I'm the mother of Riddle House."

She couldn't follow the next unfolding exactly. It was Lucie's son—a good boy. Had his degree in computer engineering and got a high-powered job in the industry. Big money, but he was working his ass off—just getting the work piled on him. And the more he did, the more they wanted out of him. Like a dog, just like a dog—they were ready to work him into the ground. Didn't have any life of his own. Worked nights and weekends. Got more and more despondent. Wouldn't tell anybody because he thought he was a failure. Started doing crack and drinking. Got sick. Got fired. Couldn't get a job.... His money, his girlfriend, his car, his apartment...

"I'm afraid," Lucie said.

Phoebe couldn't find her way out of that one either. She was overcome by the feeling that one by one each of those present in the room, each of the men and all the women, would unfold for her a tale about someone in the throes of a dilemma that went to the roots of their lives and ask her to resolve it. She'd been chosen. Queen of Gordian Knots. They'd all gotten on their Harleys and gone speeding down the interstate for the sake of emptying their minds and enjoying a little respite with a couple of drinks and music. To flow into forgetfulness. For Ralph, it was football. And there was always sleep. Precious sleep that she so longed for.

Only they'd taken their riddles with them to lay at her feet. A test. And whatever answer she gave would, for the moment, sound good and true. And they would thank her and feel grateful that she had joined their party and drunk their liquor. And then in the next moment, they would see that her answer was a flimsy thing. They'd hold it up and look at the holes and laugh. That would inspire a new riddle, more complex and imponderable than the one before. And it would go on. For now Patsy's daughter and Lucie's son seemed to have got mixed up with Helen and it didn't matter which strand you pulled, you just got all the others. The night would go on till the pile of riddles reached beyond the beyond and dissolved into a single riddle and the laughter would rise around her till she couldn't tell whether she in her failure was the source of the hilarity or whether it lay in drunken comedy of what they were trying to do.

"It can't be done." She turned to them as if that was all the light she could shed on the subject. Her pronouncement for the moment. Meaning? That you couldn't drink enough or stay drunk long enough or travel enough miles or ever travel light enough? Or that it didn't exist, that traveling light she had always hoped for, been looking for to put her faith in? Some ray touching at the edge of things. As in the dingy apartment she entered where her daughter and granddaughter lived. A student apartment, cheap enough for the fortunes of students. All her daughter's stuff lay in boxes that anonymous friends had packed for her and were taking to store who knows where and for how long. Left behind on the refrigerator was a collage Emily had made, of things drawn and cut out. A world of cats—Emily had a passion for cats. And flowers, with a great blue-winged butterfly hovering at the center. Phoebe stood in front of it, then took it down and laid it carefully in the car. She'd have that at least, the gleam of a certain potential, the sort of potential she'd seen in Helen when she was little. Had seen it, wanted to brood over and foster it in her chick. Was it love or imagination that hatched it—or both? And where did the promise go? Is that where the riddle lies—in some hidden thing?

She struggled to stand up. She tried for balance on unsteady feet. "I have to go now," she said. "If my husband wakes up..."

"It's been real nice to meet you," Lucie said, rising also. "You never did tell us about that daughter of yours. I guess we just gabbled on."

"Glad you came," she heard around her.

She walked into the coolness outside and felt a relief from the stuffiness of the room. The voices, the music fell away and she was alone again with the sensation she could never quite define but which she knew as herself. As though it all came home to that—that pulsing spark blindly aware beyond itself. She looked around with a certain wonder that she was standing there at that moment in this place. A wet fog had softened the darkness, the lights of approaching cars cutting through it briefly and vanishing like mechanical fireflies. Only the neon lights of the motel remained steady, creating a faint aura around each of the red and yellow letters.

Women Who Don't Tell War Stories

F inally the two couples came together. Over the decades they could hardly believe were gone, they kept intending to see one another; the wives dutifully sending Christmas cards, acknowledging various births, graduations, and weddings, even though the two women had never officially met. But Walt and Ralph had had World War II together: basic training at San Pedro, then duty on a destroyer escort patrolling the waters above New Guinea. Three years in the South Pacific. An experience not to be erased but one that grew ever more vivid with time.

When had they last seen one another? From the surprise of the first telephone call, they withdrew into calculation. When Walt had gotten back in '45—he'd been discharged a few months after Ralph—Ralph was just about to tie the knot. They'd flung their arms around one another, "Hey, Buddy,"—and done a few rounds of the bars in Glendale, where Ralph lived. But it was clear Ralph's mind was elsewhere: Pointed toward that long-awaited bedding with the girl who'd written him a letter every day while he was overseas. Marjorie, whose picture, the surface cracked with fine lines, he'd carried and dreamed over. While the others were losing their monthly pay at poker or dice or even cribbage, he was lost in thought above a sheet of paper—a mark of friendly ridicule from his buddies, who were confounded by what you could find to write about every day from aboard ship to a girl you couldn't even screw. Back in LA, ready to sign away his bachelorhood, he was already installed as a pressman for the *Times*, the only job he would ever hold.

Walt, on the other hand, had tried college on the GI Bill, dropped out, worked in a liquor store for a time, then had gone back to school and studied photography. He finally married Carole, after an on-again, off-again affair: a woman Ralph had disliked almost from the instant he met her—one of those high-brow, intellectual types—just before they were shipped overseas. He didn't go to the wedding, though he and Marjorie sent a nice gift of monogrammed iced-tea spoons. The couple moved to San Diego, where Walt set up as a photographer specializing in weddings.

After that first phone call—it was Ralph who initiated it, one day as he was looking at an old picture of the USS Gilligan (DE 508). The old ship, and all those who served. Then the two men swung together like magnets, on the telephone all the time—worse than teenagers, it occurred to their wives. After that, they met back and forth, sometimes in LA, sometimes in San Diego. While their friends turned to family genealogies or golf or painting in acrylics, the two men seemed to tune out all but what lent itself to the service of memory. They spent whole days at the library and in the Office of Veterans' Affairs poring over records, trying to get addresses, tracking down their surviving mates.

Their friendship reestablished, they agreed it was time to get together with the gals. Things had come full circle. Ralph and Marjorie's forty-ninth wedding anniversary was coming up. What could be better? A culminating moment, before the golden one, bringing together almost their whole lives. They made a foursome at a restaurant in La Jolla overlooking the ocean.

At first, the two women visited on one another those looks of curiosity that assess the damage the years have done and often

give rise to triumphant or invidious comparisons. But a certain sympathetic chord was struck between them immediately,
though neither could have accounted for it. They were utterly
unlike. Marjorie Calvin was a big-boned, rather dowdy woman,
with a horsy face and prominent chin, her blonde hair more
faded than gray. She was rather stiff from arthritis and moved
slowly. Perhaps that made her seem a walking apology, mount-
ing guard at the gates of her words and gestures. The other,
Carole Littleton, was a slender, dark woman, more confident
outwardly, but with a drifting gaze. They were dressed for the
occasion: the men in suits and ties, the women in their silks
and pearls. Marjorie's dress was a dark blue; Carole's a silvery
sheath. Once they were seated, and the waiter had lit the candle
at their table and told them his name was Steve, or Dudley, or
whatever, they settled into the dimness, ordered cocktails and
tried to enter the magic circle.

"Quite an occasion, quite an occasion," Ralph Calvin said,
looking around expansively. "Nice place we got here. They say
the fish is terrific." The others murmured approvingly. "Ralph's
been promising to take me here for years," Marjorie said.
Sympathetic laughter. He gave a little wave of the hand, indicat-
ing that he'd kept his promise. "Well, pal," he said, "it only took
me forty-nine years."

She had to be content with that.

"Forty-nine wonderful years," he said.

"Here's to the bride and groom," Carole said, when the
drinks came round. They clinked glasses and took a backward
glance at that post-war wedding, one of so many. Then spoke
of the kids, now grown and gone, settled into being lawyers
and businessmen, raising families. Grandchildren off at college.
Thus they surveyed the long loop of biological necessity, the
generations that would roll on past them. Or so one hoped. Past
the threats of the greenhouse effect, pollution, invasions from
outer space, whatever else of the unimaginable—and war.

They'd had their war.

"Quite a lot of water under the bridge—and I don't mean
just the South Pacific," Ralph said.

They all laughed.

"You know," Walt said. "When I think back to those days, I'm still there."

When they met now, the time that separated them from their shared experience fell away like a curtain. And though it was nothing Walt would say, they were almost closer than lovers. The eyes he looked into might have been a reflection of his own. The face of his youth, Ralph's youth, the face of all those young sailors, hastily trained in boot camp, away from home for the first time, in the midst of a war they had to feel was theirs. Roosevelt and Eleanor, and even their dog Falla proclaiming there was nothing to fear but fear itself. The long hours on watch when the waters of the Pacific moved levelly under their feet. You tended to lose yourself in that wide waste that could throw up danger when you least expected it. The fear had always been there.

Walt was a sonar-man, had been trained to a split second's response to what he saw on the screen. His eye had been needle sharp. Now he had trouble reading the fine print.

"You really got to know people," Ralph said, as he'd said so often. Packed together as they were in the bunks and the mess. Those you loved and those you couldn't stand. The smells and cigarette smoke and anxieties all, intimate as sweat; everyone's nerves connected in the same web. The officers acting like officers. The make-work and the contempt—the swabbing and polishing, the heavy weight of boredom—relieved in card games and crap shoots, nights on leave in Manila drinking themselves shitless, then going off with the whores. Only he was one of the lucky. His girl was waiting for him. They used to kid the hell out of him over those packets of letters piling up in port. How would he get caught up in time for the next batch? There was envy too. But there was a lot of stuff he never told Marjorie—it would shock the hell out of her. Even now. It was some war all right.

"You know it's a wonder we ever won that damned war," Walt said. How many times had they repeated the stories of the captain's incompetence. "I'll never forget how we ran over that Jap sub."

Carole was biting into an olive from her martini. She always demanded three olives, large ones, to soak there in the gin. She ate them slowly, measuring them out for the length of the drink, a deeply private pleasure.

"God," Ralph said. "Could anybody forget that?" He was back into the chaos, the whole ship running to battle stations, nobody knowing where the damned thing was. One of those little two-man subs. A little fish out to destroy the bigger. It was only the collision that saved them. They'd hit the damned thing because they didn't know where it was, and the Japs didn't know where they were either. Hit it and sank it. Snatched their lives out of a disaster.

And afterward, the report. The heroic dimensions of that report. They could still laugh over it, would be ready to laugh again the next time. "I told you about that," Walt said to Carole. "How he made it all up. The way they sighted the sub, calculated everything, steered the collision course."

Dozens of times. It was as though she'd lived it herself.

One story followed another. They paused for the men to order another round of drinks. There was a brief interruption to peruse the wine list, and finally to order dinner. The two women exchanged a few comments about their current situations. Marjorie still worked a couple of days a week as a laboratory technician, but she didn't like the politics at the hospital. Or the inefficiency. She'd always worked, all the time Ralph was overseas and afterwards when the kids were growing up. She couldn't imagine herself not working, though now her arthritis was severe.

Carole's attention was divided between the sympathy called for by physical ills and other misfortunes, and the men's conversation. They had gone through the episode of the suicide plane attacking the ship during the invasion of Lingayen. Fortunately it caught only a 40 mm gun tub, but four men had been killed. Walt shook his head. One of his buddies had been on the bridge. He'd never get over it, as he'd told Carole many times. That life gone—a guy he'd known, who could be sitting there right now talking about his grandkids.

The two women subsided into their drinks while their mates continued. The second round ushered the men into deeper levels of intimacy. Carole could observe the deepening fathoms, as of a submarine lowering. They'd been practicing during those trips back and forth. And now while Marjorie sipped at her martini and savored the second olive, she knew that the dining room and their presence hardly existed for the two men. Nature had given the men the edge on alcohol—it was generally the case. One drink was enough to give her a buzz—and there'd be wine. She'd have to get by on the olives. Though she'd done her share of drinking during the war. But she was younger then, working too, as Marjorie did.

She'd worked in a record store on Sunset Boulevard, a job she liked. Movie stars came in—musicians, arty types. She came to know a lot about music. About the things a small number of people paid attention to—Billie Holiday and John Jacob Niles, as well as who was big in jazz and swing. Just picked it up as she went along. And since she was a real looker then—she wasn't afflicted with any false modesty—the customers liked to have her wait on them. They took her knowledge seriously. A lot of them tried to put the make on her too. Sometimes she went out on casual dates because she was lonely. For a time, it seemed patriotic to wait for Walt to come back, though there hadn't been any promises.

She had another job on the side, writing MA theses for students in English at USC. A hundred bucks a shot. Mainly to keep herself busy. She'd never been to college—no money around for that. But she'd always read, frequently a book a day. And once she got the hang of it, doing a little research was a snap. Most evenings after work, she tucked herself in with a glass of wine and read, waking in the middle of the night to the grunting and moaning from Denise's room. The next day she got the low-down: The cutest sailor.... The most gorgeous marine.... And then you know what he did? Denise's descriptions were detailed and vivid, though, curiously she never made it to orgasm with any of the men. That didn't seem to daunt her lovemaking. Five times, can you imagine?—five times. Listen, I was worn out. Carole found herself smiling as she reached for the third olive, and looked up to catch the sort of expression from Marjorie that suggested a hesitancy to speak. The two husbands were considering the relative merits of marines and navy men.

"What are you saving yourself for—old age?" Denise kept pressing her. "Look, why don't you come with me? Look at all the fun you're missing."

What did she expect of her youth?—it was the war. And the city was caught up in it, pulsing with feverish generosity—everything for the boys. Free drinks in the bars, free rides back to base. A free-for-all. Because tomorrow you might be dead. And what did you have to lose anyway—once you knew it was your life? She felt it wherever she went, below the beat of the city, below the lull of the traffic—the whisper, Remember, there's a war on…. Remember. Remember Pearl Harbor—remember. And the headlines: the battles, the losses always there to remind you.

Finally she went with Denise. Otherwise, it was too lonely. And once you walked in the door of any bar, any dance hall, you were part of what filled the aphrodisiac air. They were all over her: she could pick any man she wanted, take him home, screw him, send him on his way. A moment of boisterous frolic, even tenderness. The little burst of the pleasure grape. Then it was over. She didn't want to see them again. There were the losers, the abusers, of course—the ones who drank too much and couldn't get it up, the ones who wanted to let go of what they'd been saving for the enemy. But she got pretty good at spotting them beforehand. She came out of it all pretty well, considering.

Now the men were mostly a blur. A few of the faces she'd kept for a time, even a few lingering thoughts. What had happened to them—had they come back? There was one she wrote to for a while. Then she didn't hear from him. She was afraid to find out what happened to him.

"They used to call it the Pearl of the Orient," Walt was saying.

Now they were talking about Manila.

"The whole city flattened." Ralph shook his head.

Not a single building left standing. The people had been destitute, starving. Whatever they got came from the rations the GI's gave them. Any female who could manage it was a prostitute. Walt had once told her how several of the guys had gone off to one of the devastated districts where they'd been told they could get it cheap. But it was hardly what they expected. A one-room hut with two old people huddled in it, and two girls, twelve or a little older—perhaps their granddaughters. There wasn't even another room, just a curtain drawn in front of a bed. "They were starving," Walt had told her. "They had nothing." "And you did it—you had sex with them?" Listen he'd told her, it didn't mean anything—it was the war. "I left them some money—we all did."

Sometimes as they lay together, her mind would float away from their intertwined bodies and she saw herself lying there like the young girl, her smooth oriental face, the eyes deep beyond her years, beyond any years.

"I know what you did during the war," Marjorie finally broke in, startling her. She had a brightness to her, as though she was about to tell some glowing thing.

The waiter, who'd somehow forgotten their salads, was now serving their entrees, and the men, their appetites opened by the alcohol, looked eagerly to their steaks. "I hope it's red inside," Walt was telling the waiter. "I hate meat that's overdone."

"Really?" Carole said to her, momentarily caught up short.

"I've been wanting to tell you," Marjorie persisted. "You roomed with Denise Albertson—she's a cousin of mine. She moved to the east coast not long after the war." Still she beamed.

Carole remembered vaguely that Marjorie had mentioned Denise from time to time in those endlessly dull notes she wrote at Christmas. She'd lost all touch with Denise, along with any real interest in her.

"We were in high school together. But I didn't see much of her. She still talks about you though. I told her we were going to meet finally." The brightness in her face suggested something not only shared, but relished.

What had Denise told her, Carole wondered, and what did she know? The two men had all but exhausted the subject of Manila. "Always wanted to go back—see it all built back up," Walt said. A pause for chewing. "I can still see the rubble," Ralph said, working the butter into his potato.

"It was an unusual time," Carole acknowledged, as something flowed back, swept over her so strongly she felt she might weep or burst into outrageous laughter. "Yes," she said, braving it out. She saw Marjorie duck her head slightly, as though a boundary existed that could be overstepped. "You were both so—" Marjorie said. "It was all so crazy. And free."

"It was the war, wasn't it," Carole said, and wondered what had really happened to her then. Or to Marjorie. She'd learned to flirt and she'd learned to dance. She could throw herself into a jitterbug, as light and fast as the best, and during the slow pieces, the palm on her shoulder blade, the man's cheek to hers, she let her body melt into pure sensation. Oh, exquisite. The moment wavering toward the next. And then the hot anticipation of the next man, always the next. No looking back. The pulsations that were in the air: she was part of all that, yet somehow on her own. That was what she brought to the man who came forward to claim her. Not that he wanted it; nor did they ever talk about how she'd spent the war. Maybe it scared him; she didn't know. And what did it matter any more? She brushed the crumbs from her lap, finished off her martini, made ready for the wine, and sliced delicately into her blackened red snapper, one of the specialties of the house.

the Death of the Cat

I.

Is it the back room where it begins, through the little passage that once held the table with the perpetual dolls' tea party, cups and saucers Lauren had since come to identify as willow ware, from Japan—connecting to the shed-like part that held two great piles, one of kindling, one of coal for the various stoves and fireplaces in the house? For the winter took its toll, and endless fires in fireplace and woodstove had to be kept stoked to keep life warm enough to get through it. Snow. *Falling in great flakes. Sticking to your coat sleeve. Wet wool smell. Snow falling and still falling, piling up to the porch, up to the very eaves, with only the chimneys poking through— Snows of all the years.* She couldn't see over the banks after her father had shoveled the walk: they made a tunnel for her to walk through.

Is the beginning there, in that dark place where the coal came tumbling in through a chute, roaring a black stream into a pile she wasn't allowed to climb on, for most certainly it would dirty her clothes—though she sneaked back sometimes and took odd-shaped pieces from the kindling heap to pound nails into? *Oh, the cat's been in the coal pile again.* There, where if you went in, you quickly came out and shut the door against the cold and the coal smell and a lingering sense of the unfamiliar; where the snow shovels leaned against the walls in the posture of waiting and the feed stood in bags for the ducks and chickens in the side yard; and where the cat had her kittens? *"I'll put a cardboard box for her in the back room. It's too cold outside. She can have her kittens there."*

Or does she enter the past by the front door, or even the kitchen door off the side porch, by way of the trellis hanging with wisteria, humming with bees and wasps visiting between the wisteria and the climbing rose at the side of the walk leading back to the garden bordered with zinnias? It is a question Lauren has been puzzling over. Her childhood has been locked away for so many years like a sealed room she never wanted to enter. Somehow forbidden, as in the fairy tales. *You may have all the keys to all the rooms, save this one. This door you must not open.* The key trembles in her hand, different from the others. Glowing now. Light from the fire has fallen on it like blood. *Fire roaring through the house like time, charring walls and ceilings, leaving black boards and cinders.* Now that there is nothing left, she circles round her childhood house. She holds up the key.

To enter by the front door would be easiest, past the porch with its swing and all the places it would go. *Philadelphia, Philadelphia and O-hi-o.* A white house with square white pillars. She stands there before the porch. An elegant house, for all it was drafty and cold. *Antebellum.* So, then, almost a hundred years old. *Antebellum, antebellum*—the words sang through her childhood and down through the years—remembered elegance. But how could it have been? Now the town she left fifty years ago sits in the backwaters of no-time, in less than elegant decay—with a modern part trying to pull away like an obstreperous offspring towards the highway sprawl that got her there. Her old neighborhood, a slum, no hint of elegance in the houses that remain. Hers is gone—not a trace, razed by a fire, in which a child died. She read this, a little news item in a newspaper all the way up in Maine, where the family had fled after the fire.

Her house where they lost their child. *Go on now, you have the key. For curiosity is the key. Curiosity killed the cat. But the cat died giving birth.*

So what is there to reclaim? She could try the various ways she'd entered the house—it was a house abounding in doors. But did it matter where you entered or what was there, or even that the cat had died? So much has gone by—in fact, a whole parade of cats. She can't remember now what the cat looked like, or even its name. Her father once spoke of a tortoise-shell cat—was that the one? Odd that even when she stood sobbing for hours, in a grief she had never known, fathomless, as though a chasm had opened under her feet, she had no real image of the cat. Was that why she wept—because she could not see her?

II.

It was Christmas, and the house quickened with the season. Not only were the doors and windows all along the street decked with holly wreaths, ending in the downtown strung with lights—so that everywhere you turned it was Christmas—but the tree was up in the living room. Excitement growing about what Santa might bring. And there was to be a party. People coming, breaking into the daily round, the familiar smell of mother-and-father presence. A different rhythm: her mother in the throes of preparation all week, she somehow always underfoot, trying to sneak a candy, or a nut, a bit of icing, a silver ball. Presents to be wrapped, hors d'oeuvres to be created, cakes to be baked: her mother trying to be everywhere at once. Eggnog—where was the recipe Mamie had given her? And hot punch—to the telephone to call Viola Foley to see if she would lend her punch bowl and cups. Could she get enough meat for the meatballs? For it was wartime, and meat was in short supply.

Bessie, the cleaning woman, came in all that week to help in the kitchen and to clean the house from top to bottom, from the arctic bedrooms upstairs with the only bathroom in the house—that guests would have to climb the stairs to use—to the living room, dining room and kitchen down below. The living room had been refurbished with a whole new set of slip-covers her mother had sewed on for months, all in a flower pattern to brighten up the sofa and chairs—it got so dark in the winter. Lights covered the tree, angel hair making green and blue and red and yellow halos around them, and glinted from colored balls and tinsel. Flames danced up from the logs set on the andirons of the fireplace. The room was set aglow—from the mahogany of her father's bookcase, where the Harvard Classics stood like soldiers pitted against the dark, to the crook of the stairs where the secretary reached up its glass-fronted shelves, on top of which the cat sometimes surveyed the whole of the living room.

Her father had come home a little early the night of the party, so that they would have time to eat and he could bathe and dress and build the fire and see to it there was enough wood to last the evening. He was in one of his rare good moods, making puns that her mother thought deplorable.

Her father was a disappointed man, Lauren now knows. Perhaps it explains why he had to ridicule people, pick flaws, bully to have his way. He was supposed to have become someone important—a doctor or a lawyer. But his own father had died when he was young and he'd had to sacrifice all his ambitions, and had never done anything more important than become president of the local Kiwanis Club and help with the annual food drive for the underprivileged. Baskets for the poor. He ran a small container factory with his brother, her uncle Melbourne, whom she'd seen only once. He was a casual fellow, "trying to be a hale fellow well met," her father said with contempt—for whom nothing was ever pressing, and who left her father all the real work, while he ran the sales end in Manhattan.

Most of the time there were quarrels in the house, as when her mother bought an extra pair of shoes or didn't cook some-thing to his taste or when he wasn't satisfied with what she did with the household money. Tonight, too, there was a little tiff. "You've got too much lipstick on," her father said.

"Good heavens, Jerome, it's no more than I usually wear."

"And rouge, for God's sake. You look like a French whore."

Her mother reddened under the comparison, so that the rouge melted in with the color of her cheeks and little sparkles came to her eyelashes. In a low voice she said, "It's our party," she said. "Why are you trying to spoil things?"

"All right, all right—do as you damned well please."

Her mother hastily wiped her eyes and went off to the dining room to get out the good dishes and the sterling silver. "They'll be here any minute."

The warmth of expectation closed round the momentary lapse, and in the kitchen Lauren had the giggles and kept dancing on her toes. She had on her patent leather shoes and a dress of tartan plaid, and imagined she was a pony. *Pony, pony, run with the wind.* Then she was a dancer, dancing with the wind. She could stay up only long enough to greet the guests; then it was upstairs to bed with her. A promise had been exacted, but she would see. There were solemnly sealed promises and negotiable promises; she had an instinct for the difference.

Then the grown-ups started coming, those great towering figures guarding the portal to the mysterious region they inhabited. First, Miss Gwen in her fur coat, and Dr. Mack, as she knew them, he, entering red-faced from more than the cold—oh that nose of his!—and cheery, shaking her father's hand, "Well hello, hello, Jerome. How's with the old boy? And this lovely girl—growing like a hollyhock, I tell you, and prettier than Shirley Temple." "I'm taking dancing lessons," she told him. "You'll be a marvel," he said and tweaked her nose as Miss Gwen took off her fur coat for Bessie to carry upstairs to the bedroom, and stood splendid in a dark blue dress dotted with rhinestones, like a night sky—with one of her famous plunging necklines. "I don't see how she gets away with it," her father would say. "Decolletage to and beyond the pale—and I don't just mean skin. How can they learn anything in front of all that cleavage?" For Miss Gwen was a high school teacher and taught math. "It's V for Victory," he would add with a laugh. She had her hair dyed as well—in Salisbury, twenty miles away, so that it wouldn't be known, but who can keep such a secret?

"The way Mack dotes on her," her mother would say, marveling.

"Like a slave," her father said. "She's tamed him and maimed him. No wonder he drinks."

"Oh, Jerome," her mother protested. "He's like a cavalier. And he knows how to hold his liquor."

"You like his style, eh? Well, don't get any ideas. He's probably too drunk to see what she looks like under all that makeup."

They never went to Dr. Mack for their dental work. "I want a man with a steady hand," her father said, "when it comes to working the drill. He could pierce a hole in your eyeball."

But she could only look at Miss Gwen in her stunning dress and take in her dark hair and her rouged cheeks and bright lipstick, all the flavor of her presence deepened by the scent of her perfume. Her heart leapt when Miss Gwen handed her the packages she'd brought, one of them a small package wrapped in a silvery paper with a splendid bow, the most beautiful package she had ever seen. It had to be hers—she wanted to tear off the wrapping right then, only it wasn't Christmas yet, so it had to go under the tree to keep company with the packages from her aunts. Dull packages with dull things inside. Useful things. Socks and panties and slips. When her aunts visited, they gave her a dime or two to buy a savings stamp to help the war effort and gave her mother advice about how to cook for her father. "Jerome can't stand a tough piece of meat," her aunt Felicia warned her. "And a sponge cake should never be heavy—you want it to melt in your mouth. It's the extra little effort in beating the eggs."

They opened the door to Mr. Ed, The Bachelor, bald as an egg, with a little rotund belly tucked under a gray wool vest. She admired the chain of his pocket watch when he took his coat off. It had a seal on it with a mermaid. His laugh tickled her. "Fussy as a woman," was her father's opinion. "Walks like he has a dime up his ass."

"How can you say things like that?" her mother would protest. "He's the nicest person in the world."

"Pfff. *Nice.*"

Lauren thought so, too, for he collected stamps and gave her his duplicates for her collection. The optometrist arrived on his crippled leg, in the company of his beautiful wife, Elizabeth, who came from money, her mother used to say in a low voice, and helped her Milman to a good thing or two. And then Miss Letty, who walked with a cane and kept a parrot.

Bessie took their coats, and her mother led her guests into the dining room and invited them to try the eggnog or take a cup of punch from Viola Foley's punch bowl. Viola herself wasn't coming—she'd called in the middle of the afternoon but had sent over her maid with the bowl. Jonathan would be there, unless he had a house call.

"I do so hope Jonathan can make it—at least for a little while. Things are so hard for him just now," her mother said.

"You're sweet on him, aren't you?" her father said. "Wish you could have married him, don't you?"

Her mother reddened. "What makes you say things like that, Jerome? Heaven knows I admire him, the way he treated Lauren when she had the grippe. No one could have been more attentive."

"You didn't pay the bill."

She kept running up to the window to be sure to see him first and greet him before her mother did. It had begun to snow again, and she could see a deeper coating on the porch. Icicles hung from the eaves. *How cold it was to put your mouth around one. But so delicious. A slice of cold that sang through your teeth.* Dr. Jonathan still wasn't in sight, but here came Jimmy Calhoun, the tallest man she'd ever seen, who'd once given her father an exploding cigar. He sold insurance. He stomped the snow off his boots.

"Well look who's here," her father said. "Didn't know you'd been invited. Well, come on in, you inverted exclamation point."

"Are you deliberately insulting me," Jimmy said, holding onto his coat, "or is that your idea of a joke?"

"Better than your idea of one," her father said, with a little laugh.

Her mother gave him a look that was both angry and pleading.

"Let me tell you one about an insurance man," Jimmy said glumly.

"Why, Jimmy, honey, we're overjoyed to see you. Now you give me that coat and come right here," her mother said. She had her hand on his arm, and he was somewhat mollified. "I want you to try some of this eggnog. If it's not the best you've ever tasted..." And she steered him into the midst of safety.

Her mother hated it when her father insulted people. "You do it all the time," she would say after the party was over. "What is it that gets into you?"

"I can't help it if they're so goddam sensitive. So what if he is a stick—can I help it? I'd just like to have a nickel for every buck he's lost on the ponies."

The party was in full swing and still Dr. Foley hadn't arrived. Sometimes her mother cast a look at the door, frowning slightly. She didn't want to set out the buffet supper until everyone had arrived and had had at least one cup of punch. The eggnog, too, had been suitably spiked. *Spiked is when you pour in the rum.* It seemed smart to know grown-ups did this. People filled the living room and the dining room, and even overflowed into the kitchen where a serious conversation was going on between the dentist and the optometrist. "But Hitler has to be stopped or all of Europe will be destroyed," the dentist said. The optometrist shifted his weight to ease his leg. "It's a bad business, though, our getting into it. All our boys getting killed and wounded." "That's war," said the dentist. "Think of what they say about the Jews, how they've been rounded up. No saying how many dead." "They're nothing to me," said the optometrist. "They've got all the money anyway. Seems like we could do with a few less of them, considering our boys are getting killed."

Dr. Foley finally arrived, stomping his galoshes on the mat and brushing the snow from his hat. "Oh, Jonathan," her mother said, as he came in bringing the cold, "I was afraid you wouldn't be able to come. I'm so sorry about Viola." Her mother put her hand on his arm. "She gets these attacks so often. I haven't seen Viola for such a while."

"Yes," Dr. Foley said. "She's been getting these migraines frequently lately. Rest seems to do the best for her. And a compress on her forehead."

"I'm sorry she has to miss all the fun."

"It's a shame," he said. "I'd hoped a party might do her good." They seemed to contemplate the fact that not only she was deprived. "I won't stay long. I just wanted to say 'Merry Christmas,' Ginny. I have some news, but it can wait a bit."

They stood smiling at one another as her father came up. "Glad to see you, Doc." The men shook hands. "Good thing you decided to take a little time off from increasing the population. Or maybe decreasing it."

The doctor laughed. "I have only a medical degree—nothing in divinity."

She stood sashaying back and forth, no one paying any attention to her. Suddenly she ran up and tagged the doctor on the arm.

"Hello, kitten," he said, and whisked her up and held her over his head and swung her down between his legs. She gave a little shriek of pleasure and begged him to do it again.

"You're still up—it's way past your bedtime," her mother said. "Up to bed immediately."

"Just a little longer," she pleaded. She knew she had an advantage, for it was a party, and nobody wanted a fuss. She loved it when Dr. Foley came to the house. Once it had been just for her, when she'd had the grippe, but more often it was for her mother, who had spells of shortness of breath.

"Now to bed," her mother said.

She pushed her advantage and made her bargain. "If I go right up to bed, can I take one present and open it up in my bedroom?"

Her mother vacillated. "Just one."

She didn't even go around and say goodnight to everyone. Forgetting to give her father a kiss, she snatched up the silvery present with the glorious bow Miss Gwen had brought and went upstairs with Bessie to help her undress. "What are you getting for Christmas, Bessie?" she wanted to know.

"Lord knows, honey—a chance to rest my feet."

"I hope you can rest your back too."

"I might try that," Bessie said, with deep laughter. "Good night, honey bun," she said. "You sleep well now. Me, I'm going home and get me some supper. I'll be back tomorrow to help with the cleaning up."

From her bed she could hear the noise from the party below, but she wasn't thinking about it. She sat with the present in her lap, turning it over and over in her hands. There in its silvery paper, it held its secret. How badly she wanted to open it. But then once she opened it, the surprise would be gone. Finally, she worked the paper loose at one end, slipped her hand along the edge and broke the two halves apart. The silvery paper slipped aside, and there was a little box. How lovely there was something else to open. Inside, on a lavender satin bed lay a slender flask of blue glass filled with perfume. She unscrewed the gold cap: Miss Gwen's perfume. She inhaled deeply—how fragrant it was. She dabbed a little behind her ears and sniffed it again. She put the cap back on. She wished everything had such wonderful scent. How lovely it would be filling the house. She imagined a whole world filled with scent.

An idea struck her. She slipped out of bed and into the hall. She could see perfectly well. A small lamp burned on the table next to her bed—the base, a dog sitting in the opening of a dog-house. The hall light was on, too, and the light in her parents' bedroom, where the coats were piled up on the bed.

She took the cap off the perfume bottle and went from coat to coat, dabbing a bit of perfume on each collar till they all smelled lovely. Then she put the cap back on. She heard someone coming upstairs and slipped under the bed, her heart pounding.

"I wish you didn't have to leave so early," her mother said.

"You know how Viola gets." It was the doctor's voice.

In front of her, two pairs of legs came down to the ankles and made feet in shoes. She could have reached out and touched her mother's high-heeled pump or run her fingers across the toe of Dr. Jonathan's heavy man shoes—but she didn't.

"Such a shame," her mother broke in. "I know you suffer."

"Ginny, dearest—there is something I must tell you."

There was a pained moment of waiting.

"There's a terrible shortage of doctors and..."

"Oh, Jonathan, you're not going?"

"I must," he said. "It would be on my conscience if I didn't."

"But we need you here. We—"

"Seltz will take over while I'm gone."

"I will miss you terribly."

"You know I love you."

Love you. Love you .

"You *will* write?" her mother said. "I couldn't bear it if I didn't hear from you—just to know you're all right."

"You know I will. And will you answer?" She heard the doctor slip on his coat. There was another pause, a low sound, almost a moan from her mother. Then she heard the creak of floorboards as they left the room and descended the stairs. She slipped out from under the bed and crept back to her own room. She lay in bed awake, the noise of the party louder than before. For a while she made caves in the covers and pretended they were inhabited by finger people. Then she rubbed her eyes and watched the little fizzles of color sail across the dark sky of her vision. Then she fell asleep.

III.

The cat, she read years later, was worshipped by the Egyptians as a goddess of pleasure. On their visits to the shrines they bought little cat mummies the way tourists buy postcards.

"When a cat rubs up against you," her father said once, "it's not showing affection for you, but taking its own pleasure. They care for no one, those creatures. Just keep them fed. Independent as hell."

"I don't see it that way," her mother said. "I think they feel affection if they're treated well."

"Pure sentimentality," her father said. "That's what I love about women—they can't think beyond their feelings. The reason they have no moral history. Can't imagine giving affection to a creature without getting something back."

She looked at him for a long moment. "That would mean frequent disappointment," she said in a low voice.

"Are you contradicting me?"

"Not at all. Or maybe you do get something back in spite of everything."

"Whatever are you talking about?"

She was lying on the floor letting the cat rub up against her head and nuzzle her face. "Don't get too close to that cat," her mother said. "They have fleas."

"She likes me," Lauren said. She loved the cat. She put her head down to hear it purr.

That Christmas she got a small phonograph you wound up and put a record on and set the needle on the edge. Each record played a song. She played the songs over and over.

> There was a jolly miller who lived on the River Dee.
> He worked and slaved from morn till night,
> No lark so blithe as he.
> And this the burden of his song
> Forever used to be:
> I care for nobody, no not I
> And nobody cares for me.

She liked the way it sounded when the phonograph was winding down, and the sound was like a gurgle deep in the throat. Years later she remembered the song. Sometimes she wondered if you could take the miller's statement at face value, or was he simply some loveless workaholic so stuck on the dollar he didn't have any friends, and was shunned by everyone. So that he had to pretend to a good thing. It was a question.

"Lauren, take that phonograph up to your room and play it there."

"Why? Don't you want to hear the music?"

"I can't hear myself think. I need to talk to your mother."

"I want some pretzels."

"In the kitchen then."

She got her pretzel and hung about the doorway without showing herself. There was trouble in the house, and she had been the cause. The day after the party her mother received a telephone call from Viola Foley. Had her husband been at the party? she wanted to know. And if he was there, what was he doing? Her mother had been taken aback. Why yes, Jonathan had been at the party, though he didn't stay long. What was the matter? The matter was the scent of perfume on his coat collar. All this with people listening in on the party line. Her mother was mystified. Perfume. It was only after she'd spoken with Miss Gwen that things came to light.

"Lauren, do you know anything about Miss Gwen's perfume?"

The bottle was empty but for a tiny drop in the bottom. She'd put it on when she was playing dressup with Janet Elsley and Suzannah Robertson, and they, too, had dabbed it behind their ears. She'd put some on her dolls. She brought the bottle to her mother. "Why that was the present for me," her mother said. "Why didn't you ask, honey? Did you put some on Dr. Jonathan's coat?"

"On all the coats. I wanted them to smell nice."

"Oh," her mother said. "Getting into mischief, I see." Yet she didn't seem angry. "Well, you did make them smell. It's a perfume that lingers. I'll have to call Viola and hope everybody that listened in the first time is listening now."

"She watches his every move," her mother said to her father the next day. "You see how innocent it all was."

"Where there's smoke, there's fire," her father said.

"What do you mean by that?" her mother said. "There wasn't even any smoke."

"Not here maybe. In any case, fires can burn without it," her father said.

"Really, Jerome, you get on my nerves."

He was determined to pick on her mother. Sometimes he did that. She could tell when he walked in the door if he carried a pick in his hand. Sometimes she hid behind his chair and popped out to surprise him. If he was in a good mood, he said, "Hello, little monkey." But tonight he was peeved, and said, "Come out of there. You're getting a little old for that."

"And what do you do in this house while I'm away all day working my ass off?"

"You know perfectly well what I'm doing—I'm cooking and cleaning, and sewing and mending. I'm keeping house and cooking your meals."

"You'd rather be off working in some factory, I suppose—being part of the war effort."

"Maybe I would."

He raised his eyebrows. "Rosie the Riveter," he said, "I can just see it. You there with all the factory girls."

"Some people believe in patriotic duty," she said. He'd put his foot down over her leaving the house and taking a job. It was a sore point both ways. Her father had tried to enlist in the Navy, but they wouldn't take him. But the doctor had gone.

IV.

It was bitter cold the night the cat died. The wind whistled around the house and through the cracks. But she didn't know about the cat. Not till she'd kept asking and asking if the cat had had her kittens. She'd been waiting for the kittens. Waiting to see them born. Waiting to see them open their eyes and lap up milk. She could dress them up in doll clothes.

But did it all happen before she and her mother went on the train? One morning her mother had packed a valise and put in some of her clothes as well. She found herself dressed in her woolen skirt and white pullover and dark blue jacket, with the blue beret she hadn't worn before. They were going some-where, on the train. Leaving the house. A cab pulled up outside to take them to the train station. Her mother sat in silence as they drove down the main street past the Sussex Hotel and the A&P and the drugstore. To the place where the stores ended and the houses began—and there was the station with its water tower set below the street just before the bridge the train went through. You had to take the stairs down. She'd held onto the iron railing. Her mother bought their tickets—to Philadelphia, and they stood waiting on the platform until the train came chuffing in. Those arriving descended. The porter took their valise, and they followed him aboard.

"Why are we going to Philadelphia?"

"To stay with your grandmother."

"When are we coming back?"

"Honey, we're not coming back."

"But what about Daddy? Isn't he coming?"

"No, he's not coming. Daddy will get along just fine."

It was strange. The train was shaking her, taking her away from her daddy and first grade. Trees, houses, people swept past. *No Daddy, no Daddy, no Daddy.* Mama and Daddy, like two pillars that held up the front porch. "How come Daddy isn't coming?" Questions. Her mother was looking pale, her eyes watery, and every once in a while she dabbed at them with a handkerchief. Then she took out her compact, applied rouge and lipstick and powdered her nose. The train kept rushing forward. *No Daddy.*

On the day after the cat died, she was standing in her mother's bedroom watching her put on her face in front of the mirror. She loved to watch her mother dress and her father shave. She liked the little brush he used to put lather all over his face, and the way the razor made a clean path through it. She adored the smell of witch hazel. She loved the way her mother brushed her hair and then wound it up into a coil and put in combs to hold it up. Her mother was going to her Saturday-afternoon bridge club, and Mrs. Langford was coming to stay with her. She didn't like Mrs. Langford because her hands were cold and limp and covered with brown spots. And she never let her do anything.

That morning she wanted to go out to the back porch to see if the cat had had her kittens, but her mother wouldn't let her. She'd whined about it during the day. Why couldn't she see? Where was the cat—why hadn't she come in? She always came inside in the morning.

"Honey," her mother said, turning to her briefly before she began to put on her makeup, "I'm sorry, but there isn't any cat any more. She died when she was having her kittens."

Died. She didn't know *died.* What was it? She strained towards explanation.

"What happened to her?"

"We don't know—she just died. That means she's gone," her mother said.

"And her kittens?"

"They died too."

She couldn't believe it. There was no way to take it in, no place prepared. "But where did she go?" The tears were coming then.

"To heaven maybe—somewhere. But now she's gone."

The tears became sobs that took over her whole body—wrenching sobs. "Why is she gone? What happened?" She was sobbing so hard she couldn't breathe. Great wails she didn't know were in her came out. She couldn't stop crying, though her eyes were raw and her nose kept running.

Ordinarily her mother would have put her arms around her and soothed her and stroked her hair and wiped her nose with a handkerchief. Only this time she stood with strained patience staring into the mirror. Finally, she turned to her and said with a sternness she didn't recognize: "The cat is gone—that's all there is to it. I want you to stop crying—right now."

V.

How long before it happened? She was a year or two older, but the war still raged on. Something was in the air, but she didn't know what it was. First it was manifest in the strained silence when her father came home from work, in the sudden outbursts from her mother, sometimes of shouting and screaming. And what had brought them about was puzzling. Once because she'd forgotten her umbrella at school. Once when she'd broken a glass. Once because she'd lost a dollar on the way to the store. The laughter was worse. Only it wasn't laughter. Just thin scrapings from where the spring had gone dry. It made her put her hands up to her ears. The quarrels had gotten worse:

why had she come back and why had he taken her back? What he'd promised and what she'd promised. And what she spent the money on. He wouldn't give her money to run the house—she'd just drink it up. Bessie would do the shopping and the cooking. Shouting and pleading. Or just shouting.

Suddenly there were other voices in the house, other presences. Her aunts, whom she'd seen once when they went to her other grandmother's funeral and twice when they came to visit. Now they were installed in the house: the ones to give her breakfast in the morning, to object if she wanted corn flakes instead of soft-boiled eggs. And when she came home from school, they were sitting over their cups of Constant Comment. Her aunt Felicia, who looked like a spoon, with skinny arms straight as rulers; and her aunt Flo, lumpy as a feed sack. They both looked like her father, with his nose and chin, but with pale blonde-white hair instead of black. His nose made for a strong face, but on the women it left little space for beauty.

They were women who knew the value of a dollar and whose sense of utility was like the starch they gave to their dresses. Bessie was sent away, and the two of them shopped and mopped and cooked and mended and ironed her dresses and plaited her hair. It was as though the day came mounted on a little wheel they had to keep from jumping off the track and crashing in a heap. She learned never to ask about her mother; she continually caught hints of her existence though seldom of her reality.

I always thought Jerome could have done better. She had a wandering eye, that one.

She didn't know her mother had an eye problem. Her aunt Flo was always telling her to stop squinting and to move over into better light to read.

Jerome said her hand was on the arm of every man she knew. More than friendly. And then, of course, the letters. I hope Jerome burned them.

She didn't know when or how she knew that Dr. Jonathan had been killed in the war: he'd been trying to get to a wounded G.I. during one of the battles in North Africa. Or whether his death had begun or hastened her mother's dissipation. Or where she was left on account of it. She saw less and less of her father, who was now down in Washington, for things were getting worse on the production end of the business.

There were shortages of materials, and he was hoping for a government contract.

"What do you want to be when you grow up?" her aunt Flo once asked her.

"A dancer," she said, even though her lessons had been stopped.

"You'd do better to learn some secretarial skills," her aunt said. "Dancers starve to death."

It was her first real experience of hatred. But she never saw things the way her aunts saw them. Certain images she clung to all down the years, stubbornly, as though claimed from the last vestiges of fading sight, where things blur into confusion. She saw her mother sitting in front of the mirror brushing her hair, twisting it into a roll and pinning it up on her head. The rich chestnut color—the way her hair caught the light when she entered a room, as though something inside her had turned it on. Her features she couldn't be certain of. She had only a single photograph, of her mother as a young girl before she was married.

There was another image, perhaps more crucial. She was left with that puzzling moment on the platform after they'd descended from the train. For they never got to Philadelphia, no more than the porch swing had taken her there. They were to change trains at Wilmington. She had hold of her mother's hand and was still asking questions as her mother picked up the valise and they began walking toward the station. They were caught up in a crowd of people, porters bustling around them. It was fearfully noisy. Then the pace of her mother's walk changed, as though intention had gone out of it. She sensed bewilderment or loss of nerve. Her mother paused, opened her purse, and pulled out a train schedule. "Where are we going now?" she asked.

"It's all right," her mother said. "There's another train. We'll get home in time for supper."

A sense of some terrible wrong seized her. More than disappointment. "Why? Why are we going back?"

"Who would be there in that empty house?" her mother said distractedly. "Who would feed the cat?"

Cochise

Even with the auction coming up—posters all over town—Joel had trouble persuading himself the ranch had indeed been sold. The Shelton Ranch, in the family since the 1860s. It was a painful ending to the months of wrangling among the brothers—his father and four uncles—during which Joel had maintained the desperate hope they'd come to an agreement and somehow keep the ranch. No use, finally. It was sold with all its history. Saturday he'd go out to the ranch one last time before the new owners took over. There he'd see all his grandmother's things, and those that had come down to her, displayed on the lawn for public view—the furniture and the old piano, the knickknacks and keepsakes—ogled and picked over by strangers. He'd managed to snag a family album with photographs he prized—he was a photographer himself—and there were other things he wanted, if he could afford them. Some notable items had already been sold off privately to dealers and collectors; others had been taken by his kinfolks.

He didn't want to go out there alone, to face whatever family members might show up, neither those who were as disappointed as he, nor the others, including his father, who'd been the most eager to pitch into the money. An ally, who wouldn't even know he was one—another voice in his ear—was what he needed.

"How about going out to the ranch with me this Saturday," he said to George Lee, his buddy at the local college, where both worked on the maintenance crew after classes. Joel was older, almost twenty-seven, come back to college after various efforts and failures.

"You really ought to see the place." They were sweeping among the stacks in the library, with its musty smell of old books. "If you haven't been on any of the ranches around here, it's an opportunity. I can show you around." He'd fallen into his old enthusiasm. "You can follow the creek all the way down the canyon—it's special. I once found an axe-head there, and lots of arrowheads." An appeal to George's Native American blood.

He told him about the times, as boy and man, he'd taken a horse out for the day, with a lunch his grandmother had packed for him, and how, after a day of rocks and the river, he came back feeling lucky to be alive.

"You get out there on the land and it's like you remember something you were meant never to forget."

George looked skeptical. "I don't mind a good hike once in a while, but I can do without the horses. Now that I've got my Harley, I've got all the transportation I need." He grinned. Often enough Joel watched him shooting off on his motorcycle, Nancy or Penny or Jessie perched behind him, hands around his waist. His greatest thrill, he told Joel, were those hands, with one of the girls sitting thigh to thigh. He was a handsome, cheerful fellow, stocky and well-muscled. He'd come to college to play football, but a knee injury had taken him out for the duration. He still had hopes of becoming a coach.

"A Harley won't take you there."

"Man, it'll take me any place I want to go."

"I thought you Apaches were into horses," Joel kidded him.

"Not this Apache—too much other stuff got mixed in along the way, if it ever got mixed. Red blood and white blood and Mexican blood. Sometimes I think there's a war going on in my blood." He left off sweeping. "Anyway, I got a cousin on my mother's side who was into rodeo stuff. Great on a bronc; even got bucked into the prize money a time or two—'til he broke his leg."

"Cochise and his warriors used to come through our ranch," Joel added. "He used to take water from the well, water his horses."

"Yeah? A wonder he didn't kill the lot of you."

"Apaches did kill one of my great-uncles and a young boy. The rest were lucky, I guess. My grandmother told me her mother saw Cochise once when she was just a girl—came out to the well and just saw him standing there. She didn't run. She just said, 'That's all right—take all the water you want.' And then he disappeared. Later she found out he was dead—it was his ghost."

"Look, don't give me that stuff," George said, waving his hand in front of him as though to ward it off. "I don't believe in it. Maybe she was making it up."

"I never thought so," Joel said. "You've never seen an ancestor?"

"Hell no, and I don't want to. The past is dead—I'm alive. Let me live my life my own way. I got enough troubles as it is."

"Tell me if you ever do," Joel said.

"Sure I will." George laughed. "You've been poking around too much in these stacks instead of working—I know you."

It was true. Sometimes he'd take a little break if his eye lit on a title that drew him to the shelf and the book proved to be especially compelling. He'd read a good deal about the local history. Always there were ghosts. La Llorona, the weeping woman—many stories about her. He'd never seen a ghost himself, but he couldn't say he didn't believe in them. He'd never thought his great-grandmother was making it up. It was a story that had come down in the family.

He'd studied the pictures of General Crook and Kit Carson, most particularly the great Indian leaders—Geronimo and Mangus Coloradas—looked into their eyes and tried to get into their bones. Especially Cochise, with his connection to the ranch—who'd fought his losing battle with such skill and tenacity and who was said to have been a man of great integrity.

"You're part Apache, and it was Apache land," Joel said. George shrugged. "What do you want to go digging for into all that old dust?"

"I don't know," he said. "It's pretty interesting." Even after he knew something, he was never sure what he should make of it. He'd learned that at the start Cochise hadn't wanted to make war against the white man. Then came the Bascomb affair, when Cochise had been falsely accused of kidnapping a young boy and had been taken prisoner along with family members. Cochise later escaped. One thing led to another: refusing ransom for his prisoners, Bascomb had hanged captives from Cochise's family, at the same time Cochise had tortured and killed prisoners he had wanted to exchange. Then the searing hatred and acts of revenge, the terrible things both sides had done to each other for twelve years. Joel didn't know what to do with it, but somehow it all seemed to belong to him.

"You ever looked at any good pictures of Cochise?" he said. "I know a book if you haven't."

"Of course I've looked at him," George said. "You think you invented him? It's what my step-dad used to call me when he thought I was getting too ornery."

Joel let it drop. "You want to go out with me?"

George paused, studied him. "Okay. Penny's on for Saturday night. But the afternoon—okay. I got nothing better to do."

When they got there, on George's motorcycle, the road was lined with cars and trucks, people coming early to view the many items. Everything was set up—a woman at the cash box handing out numbers, the auctioneer testing the microphone. A table with food, soft drinks and coffee was set off to one side. Joel saw that the mobile homes housing the families of his uncles Walton and Ajax were gone—moved into town. The ranch had been their life, even though they'd taken their knocks, what with the drought, the price of feed, the winter losses, the dips in the cattle market. He didn't see any of his uncles or their families, but his father was there.

"Pretty nice spread," George said, surveying the house set back among the cottonwoods, the stretch of grassland. "The land looks pretty good here."

"When there's rainfall," Joel said, "there's good grass." They walked in the direction of the furniture lined up on the lawn.

Now that it was all pulled out of the rooms it had inhabited and its context stripped away, it was, in his eyes, just a collection of worn, even shabby, objects. Something essential was gone. And the rooms themselves would be bare and stark. He had no desire to go inside the house and hear the floorboards creak as he crossed them. He ran his eye over the beds, the mattresses, the dressers. He saw that the little dresser his grandmother used wasn't among the bedroom furniture—his Aunt Ella had very likely claimed it. But there was her little gilt mirror. Let him buy that at least.

"Why, Joel—good to see you, son." He glanced over to see Nora Matthews, who'd taken care of his grandmother during her last illness. Though she was small and thin, her presence held a strength Joel found comfort in. His grandmother had been in good hands. He was fond of Nora.

"I just want to get some little thing that belonged to your grandmother," she said. "I see some dealers—I hope things don't go out of sight. I'd love to have her sewing basket."

They should have given her that much at least, Joel thought. "I'd like to get that little mirror," Joel said. "It was her mother's."

After exchanging bits of news, Nora asked him how his photography was coming. "You do take wonderful pictures, Joel. I saw that one of yours in the newspaper. We'll see you in the Sunday magazines one of these days."

"Thank you, ma-am." He'd won an honorable mention in a national competition and had done a couple of local assignments, but it would be a while before he made any real money. He still had a year of school to finish and loans to pay off. His father had told him it was time for him to earn his own way.

"Well, you keep on," she said. "It's always a struggle at first."

Joel went over to where George was examining some tennis rackets on one of the tables.

"That's my father over there talking to the auctioneer," he said to George. "We don't exactly see eye to eye."

"Join the club. Neither do I and my step-dad."

Joel's father wasn't the only one who wanted to cash in on the ranch. Let's face the facts, he was fond of saying. "Hell, we'll just about go under with the damn taxes." Plus there was no money in ranching these days unless you had a spread half the size of the county... And there was all that Hollywood and Texas money out there just waiting. Sooner or later some celebrity was bound to come along, itching for a tax write-off. Why the ranch could become a show place in the right hands.

"Well, don't get bitter," George said. "You've got your life ahead. Things change."

"Come over this way. I'll show you the orchard and back of that is the well."

The auction was starting up. The bigger pieces would go first—they probably had a good hour before they started on the smaller items. "Howdy, folks," the auctioneer said. "Glad to see so many of you here with us today. We got some mighty nice antiques—furniture and dishes your kids and grandkids'll wrassle you for."

The two of them paused at the food table for a couple of hot dogs and soft drinks, then walked around the side of the house toward the back, where the apples were ripening. Some had fallen to the ground. Joel picked a couple and gave one to George. "They've had to put in new trees one time and another," Joel said, "but this one over here was my grandmother's pear tree. She was so proud of it. I can't tell you how many times I climbed that tree picking pears. Sweetest pears I've ever eaten. It doesn't really bear any more."

He'd taken various pictures of the trees, in blossom and with ripening fruit. The pear tree was his favorite. Even when his grandmother was in her seventies, she'd climb up on a ladder and pick the fruit, despite the admonitions of her sons. From around front the auctioneer's voice fell into its patter, and Joel listened for a moment as things were going, going... He and George stood against the trees, eating their hot dogs, drinking their sodas.

Then he took George back by the well. "They had to dig it deeper once during a drought, put in new casing and a pump, but it's always had water," Joel said. "Good water too. Now everything's all modern—bathroom and kitchen, with a holding tank up there. Made things a lot easier."

They left the orchard, crossed back behind the corral, the stable and sheds and moved down toward the creek bed, dry now, lined with cottonwoods. "If there's rain, it really rushes along. Sometimes I used to take a sleeping bag and just lie out here under the stars." They hiked deeper into the canyon. "There's a cave up there." Joel pointed it out. "I think it was an Indian hideout once upon a time."

"Can we go up there?" George said, suddenly interested. "I've always had a thing for exploring caves."

"You go ahead," Joel said. "It's not very deep—no place you can fall into. I'm thinking I'd better head back. I don't want that mirror to go."

"Sure—I can find my way."

He left George and hurried back to the auction. They were beginning on the lamps and smaller items. One of the antique lamps, which had hung over the dining room table, brought a round of eager bidding and finally went for what would have been a month's salary. Not that he was paid all that much.

He could go a couple of hundred for the mirror. The opening bid was fifty dollars, and there were several on it immediately—a couple of dealers, four women and himself. "Two hundred," he was saying, almost before he could catch his breath. Then it was two-fifty. He didn't let go, even though he was getting beyond his depth. Finally he quit at three hundred. To his surprise Nora took up where he left off, and bid with such tenacity that first the dealers, and then the women dropped out. At four hundred sixty-five, it was hers, and he rejoiced that she had won out.

A few minutes later she was holding the mirror out to him. "I bought it for you," she said. "I just knew you had to have it. Wouldn't have been right otherwise."

"But Nora—"

"Don't say a word," she said. "If ever I'm in need, you'll come to my rescue—I know you will. So that's that. Now I'm going to buy that sewing basket."

"Well—" he said, overcome, hardly able to gather words to thank her. "I'll pay you back," he said.

But she waved him off. "You just go on taking pictures," she said, and went back to her place to wait for the sewing basket.

He stood holding the mirror as if he didn't know what to do with it. His face stared back at him solemnly, as though that was all it could show him. Too bad it couldn't have recorded something of the life that had passed in front of it—like a camera. At least he had the photograph album. He wondered what he could collect from some of his kin. . .

"I see you got Mama's mirror." His father was standing there in front of him, a tall slouching man with a ruddy, weathered face.

"Nora bought it for me."

"I saw. Mighty kind. You speaking to me now?" his father said.

"I was never not speaking to you," Joel said. "We just didn't see things the same."

"Walton isn't speaking to me," his father said. "Nor Ajax. Harry didn't give a damn, and Dexter's all eager to expand his car business. I guess that was two for and two against—one on the sidelines. Hell," he said, "they've both got Ag. degrees—they'll be in demand. It isn't as if they got left in the lurch."

Joel thought of what his grandfather had said just before he died. "I know you boys aren't going to give a damn when I'm gone—probably aren't listening to me now. But don't sell the ranch—a man's rich when he's got land."

It occurred to him that he was part of the living memory of the place. And if he got things written down, there might be something of a history. The notion cheered him.

"I loved this place, dammit. Only sometimes you have to let go."

But his father was always letting go—maybe he didn't know what to hold onto. He and Joel's mother had split up when Joel was two, leaving him to be brought up by his grandparents. Now his father was hauling feed and supplies locally, trying to make a go of that. He'd have some money now, but it wouldn't be all that easy for Walton and Ajax to start over—men in their mid and late fifties, who'd spent their lives on the ranch. Joel wondered if they'd ever forgive their youngest brother. Another schism in the family—that was part of its history now. And where did that leave him? Right now Joel couldn't answer the question.

"You know," his father said uneasily, "I can give you some money now. Help you get through school, set up a dark room in your own place."

"I'll think on it," Joel said. His father had never been all that sold on his photography—thought he ought to go into computers and make some real money. "Right now I'm not needing anything—" He could see a hardening around his father's mouth.

It occurred to him he'd have to get home with the mirror. He'd never make it back on George's motorcycle. "—except maybe a ride home."

"I can handle that," his father said. "But I'll have to settle up with Oscar after this whole shebang is over. That'll be a while. Here, take the keys and put that thing in the truck."

"I'll find George," he said, "and tell him he can go on back without me."

He put the mirror in the front seat of the truck and started back towards the canyon. He saw George hurrying toward him as though he couldn't get away fast enough. "Boy, am I glad to see you," George said, catching his breath.

"What's the matter? Something happen?"

"I don't know," he said. "I just got into that cave and had this spooky feeling—I had to get out of there."

"Did you see anything?" Joel said, excited.

"No, I didn't see anything—only there was a shadow on the wall. It wasn't anything. It was like I was seeing things." His voice was growing hoarse.

"Did it look like anybody?"

"Look, nothing happened," he protested. "You got me into this state—all this talk and shit. I dreamed something in front of my eyes—I made it up out of my head."

"It's okay," Joel said, trying to calm him. He could feel George's agitation. "Let's just go on back."

"Why do you want to go looking for ghosts?—it's crazy, man. Who knows if they bring good or harm? Why look for trouble?"

Maybe you get it anyway, Joel thought, just from not knowing. They walked in silence for several minutes. Finally Joel said, "Maybe you're missing an opportunity."

"Opportunity for what?" George said scornfully.

"Maybe he's there so you'll look at your native past."

They were approaching the parked cars. "I'm out of here."

"You don't have to worry about me," Joel said. "I'm riding back with my dad—I've got the mirror to lug."

"Well, good. Otherwise you'd have to walk."

"I'll buy you a beer," Joel said.

"Better make it two."

George took off in the direction of his motorcycle, and Joel stood watching his determined stride. The auction was still going full tilt, but he wanted no part of it. He still had a little time. And he thought of what he needed to do before he left. He wandered slowly back to the orchard and then to the well. He looked down its mossy sides to the water. Then he pumped some water into a pail, cupped his hands and drank. The rest he poured out on the ground. "Water your horses," he said, standing up straight. "Take all the water you want."

the Orange Bird

The crate from Spain, long awaited, arrived at the gallery that morning. Mildred was all agog, a kid getting a birthday present, hovering over Mark as he cut the wires and pried up the planks. Carl and Antonia stood by, witnesses of the grand opening. She'd been on pins and needles for months— would the shipment arrive, would Diego come through? This was her baby. She winced as the nails came out, as though Mark might damage something, and it would be hell to pay if he did. He worked loose the lid, took out the packing. A blast of color struck him in the eye. Careful of the baby, he lifted the top canvas and set it up on a chair. The four of them stood back appraising. There it was: a vase of red and yellow flowers like fried eggs, a drape to one side; in the background an amorphous mauve shape next to what could have been a corner of the Alhambra. In front, a lobster, cooked and coral. On the other side, a basket with clusters of grapes spilling out, two apples in the neighborhood, an orange bird behind. As a finishing touch, the surface offered a crackled effect. Breathtakingly awful.

"It's beyond imagination," Mildred enthused. "Just look at the color."

Mark caught Antonia's eye, but her expression was neutral. "You can certainly see the Spanish touch," she said. He covered his mouth to avoid some expression of horror, to still the laughter that threatened to double him over. Mildred shot him a glance, dismissed him. If she'd caught his disloyalty, it didn't matter.

"Well, Diego's really done me proud," Mildred said, turning the paintings over to Carl, who did most of the framing. Eleven more lay in the crate, looking as though they'd been cranked out by a machine. "A black frame," Carl said, "to lock in the color. Or maybe silver." Carl, expert at measuring and cutting, never had an opinion about anything he was asked to frame. Just so there were no complaints from the customer. Antonia was a different kettle of fish.

"I'm just thrilled," Mildred said. "It's so hard to get a still life that'll go over. People get bored with the same old stuff. I've seen too many pumpkins in my time. I've got to call the Steens." She went off to do so at once.

Thrilled. To have hit upon Spanish kitsch instead of the mere domestic species, no doubt offering employment to how many struggling, or maybe not-so-struggling, Spanish artists.

"Thrilled? She can't believe that's art," Mark said to Antonia after Mildred had left for the bank. "It belongs in Wal-mart."

"Does it matter?" She was a small energetic woman in her fifties, a photographer, who supplemented her income by working part-time in the gallery and by doing weddings. She liked the connection. She and Mildred had been on friendly terms for years. A few prints of her photographs, studies in light and shadow, offering haunting contrasts, hung on the walls, attracting an occasional buyer. To Mark, these were the best work in the gallery. "Believe me, Mildred knows what she's doing. She's had to learn the hard way."

He tried for a title. "'The Afternoon of the Lobster Quadrille.'—how does that grab you?"

"It's a pretty inert lobster."

"A more Daliesque approach? 'The Cornucopia's Lament'? 'Sancho Panza Strikes Again' or 'The Persistence of Indigestion'?"

"You haven't quite caught the essence. It has a certain genius," Antonia said, cocking her head, as though to capture it more fully. "A genius of badness—that's hard to come by."

"I think Mildred's outdone herself."

Transcending the typical, the banal, the decorative, this was their bread and butter. Landscapes of houses and trees decked in summer green; seascapes with foam, and sometimes dramatic clouds; the snows of a New England winter—the "yesteryear stuff," he called it—what would go well in a dining room or over the mantel of a fireplace. Technical skill to the grommet. ("Don't knock it," Antonia said. "Considering the way they come out of some of the art schools these days. Can't draw for shit—" "I don't." he insisted.) Still anybody could have painted them. No character, no signature. Early Motel. Late Professional Building. For the suburban nests of the up and grasping, fine for bank or doctor's office. It didn't offend—maybe even convinced people there was a place for art. For artists. For himself—or so he hoped.

He figured he'd hit it lucky when Mildred took him on his first year out of art school. Except for the one or two who'd landed on their feet, who'd somehow gotten connections and were consistently selling their work, most of his buddies had either gone into advertising or some form of computer graphics. A wonderfully talented water colorist was taken on by a greeting-card company. Left to his own devices, he'd managed to cobble together various part-time jobs. For a time, he worked nights in a bakery, after which he threw himself exhausted into bed. Then the gallery job opened up, offering him a glimpse into the art scene and actually allowing him time to paint on his own. For the moment, at least, he felt he was struggling in the right direction. If most of the stuff Mildred sold was nothing he'd ever paint himself, at least he didn't have to think about it. His work there was varied enough to be interesting: talking to potential buyers, trying to connect them with what they were looking for, whatever it was, or else setting up the shows. These were often the work of artists who combined fabric and flower arrangements, did playful treatments of animals, or water colors of river, lake, and rocky abutment. Occasionally Mildred took in a painter who moved in the direction of abstraction or did something unusual with color. He'd hung a couple of shows that moved toward the pretty good.

So far the only work that genuinely interested him was Antonia's photographs. When he tried to tell her how good they were, her face reddened, as though he'd discovered a secret that couldn't bring her any benefit. "I'm very grateful to Mildred," she'd say, as though her talent was owing to her as well. "She actually has one hanging in her living room."

Her first years Mildred had taken up young and promising artists and given them shows, even though their work mostly didn't sell, and more than once she'd been left in the lurch. She hadn't done that for quite a while, but had subsided into success. She had, in fact, hit the jackpot several years back when she'd been the one to handle the contract for the paintings and assorted art objects for a cluster of condominiums going up. A number of artists both in the area and outside had been commissioned to do paintings, even a few sculptures, suitable not only for living and dining rooms, but for bedrooms and hallways. Mildred had made it into a real competition, had worked up a lot of publicity in the papers. Artists had submitted slides for the project, and Mildred had made the selections. They'd filled up the place with beach scenes at sunrise and sunset, flower arrangements, birds in flight. Pinks and peaches, vibrant greens and blues, and lavenders going from sultry to misty. The impression apparently, was to make the Midwestern city dweller believe he'd been transported to Florida. "Mildred made a bundle," Antonia had told him. "Really expanded her collection. You should see that place of hers."

By all descriptions a real showplace. Expensive woods, stone fireplace. One of the best private art collections she'd seen in the city. Not just prints and ceramics by Matisse and Picasso—the Names—but lithographs by Romare Bearden, paintings by Wayne Thiebaud, Alice Neel, Chuck Close, and other notables. Work that took not just money—apparently she had plenty to throw around—but an eye too.

Mildred was a puzzle to him. Her little-kid excitement over the hopelessly bad see-sawing with her aim to live with the good stuff. For investment purposes? To show she had class? She knew how to make a buck—you had to give her that. But beyond that? He wanted a way past equivocation, to where their sympathies might join—especially when she said just before the shipment arrived, "Hey, what are you painting these days? I'd like to see your work."

He was flattered, yet reluctant, at the same time curious to see what her response might be. Actually, he felt pretty good about what he was doing. He hadn't found an approach that satisfied him; he was still trying to break loose from the school stuff he'd done, mostly abstract expressionist displays with heavy impasto and a lot of surging shapes, work that now struck him as turgid and derivative, whatever praise he might have received. Now he was working into a more figurative mode, trying to use color with more finesse. After a long love affair with the German expressionists, Bonnard had become his idol.

Then she mentioned it again. "When are you going to bring something in?" When he did, taking in half a dozen of his recent canvases, Mildred set them up along the wall, regarded them with a critical eye. "You're working out of the dead stuff," she told him. "That's good." Hardly the enthusiasm that met the Spanish still life, but better than nothing. "Keep moving. Bring some more when you get them done."

He couldn't help an occasional fantasy—her giving him a show, inviting him to her house to see her art work... All very unlikely, he told himself.

"Twelve of them," he said to Antonia. "How in the hell can she sell twelve of those? Impossible."

"You want to bet on it," Antonia said, giving a little ironic smile.

"Okay," he said. "You win, I'll buy you a beer at Stefanel-li's."

"If I lose?"

"I'll buy you a beer anyway." If he could manage it. Right now he was pressed from all sides—student loans, a car going bad, a nagging weakness in the chest he hadn't yet taken to a doctor.

She laughed. "You're on. Only if you win…"

"Trade me one of your photographs for one of my paintings."

"A deal. You look like you could use some coffee. I'll make some." She moved toward the back.

"Thought it was my turn."

"You can do it next time."

He was bone tired. He'd stayed up most of the night working on a painting that refused to jell. Tonight he'd take a break, head off to Stefanelli's and sit around with the old Italian men still in the neighborhood who frequented the place. For some reason he felt more at home with them than with the young guys that hung around. They were no longer trying to prove anything—a relief. Especially if you had everything to prove yourself. It was his only social life, as much as he could afford. As it was, he made barely enough to pay the rent on an apartment in a rundown, blue-collar neighborhood, the living room serving as his studio. He'd rigged up a set of lights so he could work nights after he got home. Usually Mark managed a couple or three hours of painting, but sometimes stayed up 'til all hours when he really got going. He dared not do it often—he couldn't risk falling asleep on the job. He lived for his two days off, Sunday and Monday, when he could work uninterruptedly, sleeping late and working all day. He'd lost touch with most of his college friends. When one of them called, he was eager enough to talk on the phone but was vague about future meetings—at least for the time being. To all intents and purposes, he'd gone into hibernation. He had work to do, had to see what was in him.

The first of the Spanish still-lifes sold the next week. It was just what the Steens wanted. He drew a quick sketch of them in the little book he carried in his pocket: a large, hearty woman with graying hair, who wore huge earrings with smiley faces, and her balding mate, who spoke in quick explosive bursts: "Terrific color—light up that north wall come winter, won't it, hon? Terrific color."

"I was sure you'd like it," Mildred said.

Antonia gave him a significant look. Okay, one down. Mildred hung up a second and sold it the same week, this time to a woman who came in with a handsome full-size poodle. The sketches became a series, expanding like a rogues' gallery. As a preface, he'd written, "What do these faces have in common?"

After the eleventh had sold, in less than three months, Mark conceded that he owed Antonia a beer. That is, if he could afford it. He'd just gotten his car out of the shop, the eighteen-year-old TransAm he'd taken over from his uncle. Twelve hundred bucks on his credit card, not to mention the interest. The zeros on the bill haunted him. More out of desperation than hope, he decided to ask Mildred if she'd give him a show. His work was taking shape; it had some flashes here and there. If he could sell a few paintings...make a small debut. He went back over her responses as though he were counting credits. "Nice color going there." "The shapes in that one—very organic." Had anything impressed her?

He approached her at her desk cluttered with catalogs and brochures, the last Spanish still life emphatically occupying the wall just behind. She looked up from a catalog she was examining.

"An exhibit?" he asked.

"Old friend of mine from school," she said. He drew up to look over her shoulder, while she turned the pages. Mountains, cactus-studded landscapes, horses. Portraits of Hispanics. Nothing new, but genuinely well done. "She's got something," he said, leaning forward to read the name. Heather Duncan.

"A lot of talent. She used to do things like you'd see in a dream. I've got one in my bedroom. Went out to Santa Fe a few years back. Now they're selling everything she paints. Yeah," she said, "she's finally done it."

"Some great artists have gone out there to New Mexico. Such a powerful landscape."

She didn't seem to hear him. "All she needs are a few cows' skulls."

"You going out for the opening?" he said, feeling some idiotic need to put off what he wanted to ask her.

"Too many things pressing," she said.

Then she said. "Sit down. There's something I've been think-ing about. I just wanted to be sure it was the right moment."

His heart took a sudden leap, even as the Spanish still life met his eye and the orange bird seemed to stare right through him.

"Can you paint one of these?" she asked him, gesturing to-ward the painting.

You've got to be kidding, he almost blurted out. He was struck dumb. "Nobody's ever asked me," he said.

"I'm offering you a chance," she said. "There are lots of young artists around who could use the money."

Including himself. "Well, I…"

"Of course you can," she said, suddenly beaming at him. "I know you can—I've seen your work. Two hundred apiece," she said, "plus," she added indulgently, "an allowance for canvases and paints. I want another twelve of them."

Enough to get himself out of hock and have a little to float on. Would it be selling his soul? But then, maybe he could actu-ally learn something, improve some of his techniques. Like the apprentices in the old days. The idea was beginning to appeal to him. "I'll give it a whirl," he said.

"Good boy," she said. "I knew you had it in you."

He spent the next Sunday stretching and gessoing canvases. He'd brought home the still life and hung it up on the wall, where, with the lights on it, it gave off an unholy garish sheen. He planted himself in front of it and tried to figure out the colors. Mix and match. When in doubt, lay on the cadmiums. Orange, red, yellow. After his initial drawing and painting classes, his struggling beginner's efforts, he hadn't done any close copying. But he figured he'd go about it the way he'd seen it done in the text books: make a grid, block out the forms, sketch in the details, set up some good background colors. Since this was a production job, he could try laying-in the larger ar-eas, moving from one canvas to another. He did the drape, the slab of building, the ambiguous mauve shape, then back to the first, working toward the more challenging objects. The flowers he found monstrously difficult—gaudy, truculent, but somehow elusive, innocent even in their vulgarity. He thought of Mildred. He had to keep the colors clean, pay attention to the parts but not neglect the whole. In its way, it all had to work—flowers, basket, grapes, apples, lobster, bird. As Antonia suggested, there was a certain genius in it. You had to find your way into that, on the terms it demanded. Harder than he thought—more time-consuming than he expected. For when he got through the first, the painting stood inert before his eyes. Still life indeed—nature morte. So what was wrong?

Every night he came home from work and after a quick supper—a sandwich, a can of soup heated up, or a frozen pizza he popped into the oven—he approached the painting with a certain dread, while the rest stood lined up against the wall. For two or three hours he tried to meet it on its own terms. He had to wipe away any trace of a smirk, humble himself; otherwise it wouldn't yield. Sometimes he wanted to weep with vexation—the damned thing wasn't worth the effort. Then one night when he'd almost despaired, it all came together. Just like that, as though something had sneaked in when he wasn't looking. He worked in a frenzy till four in the morning. Then it was finished, sweet Jesus—it was done. He collapsed into bed but couldn't sleep, fueled awake by a curious sort of excitement, even triumph. When he finally awoke from an exhausted sleep, he had to go immediately to look at the painting. It held, cohered, made a world, out of which the orange bird met his eye with a certain fierce partiality, seemed to follow him around the room, as though he'd somehow claimed it. He couldn't bear its gaze.

"Perfect," Mildred said, when he took it in. "Absolutely perfect. Look at this, will you," she said, calling over Antonia. "I think you've even improved on it. Those flowers have a certain subtlety." She considered. "Maybe with the rest you could give the bird just a few more touches." He didn't know whether to laugh or weep.

The subsequent paintings went more quickly. Mildred thought it best that he work from his own copy rather than the original. Let there be a few distinctive touches, so long as the painting had the same impact. He was learning quickly, discovering something from each one. Now that he'd got the colors down, he began to work up a kind of shorthand, laying in some of the areas almost without thinking. He'd got the flowers under control; the grapes had taken on a kind of fullness, as though they might explode into flavor on the palate. The apples, too, more and more appealing, were almost seductive. Now it was the bird that gave him fits. What was it doing there in its orangeness? Was there such a creature? Or a figment of dream caught in a landscape it too found unreal?

Now he painted in his dreams as well as his waking hours, painted endlessly in a kind of Sisyphean labor, so that he was more exhausted when he woke than when he went to sleep. Sometimes he was in an undersea realm, trying to paint a lobster as it disappeared in a mass of undulating bodies and snapping claws. Sometimes he found piles of wormy apples he had to sort through to find the two he needed to paint. And many a night he spent looking for the orange bird, who continually eluded him, at times leaving behind a single glowing feather. The bird challenged him in some uncanny way, and just when he'd given it up, it would appear for an instant, remote and formidable. On one occasion it landed on his shoulder, its voice in his ear, almost a human voice, but so gentle and caressing, it seemed more than human. When he woke, he felt he had gained something of incomparable value, though what he couldn't have said. When he looked at the painting, the bird confronted him as imperiously as ever, returning only his stare; and could it have uttered a sound, he would have expected a voice harsh as a crow's. From the finished canvas its eye followed him relentlessly around the room.

He wanted to be rid of its dismaying presence, wanted to be done with the whole ungodly mess. He worked as though under sentence, as though he'd entered a dimension where his dreams were part of the trial. Even as he brought in the canvases one by one, to Mildred's extravagant praise, he had no sense that he was emerging from his predicament. Then when he brought in the twelfth—they had been selling almost as quickly as he could paint them—she said, "I want a dozen more."

He broke into a sweat. *It's killing me*, he wanted to protest. His mind leapt into consequences and options. She might can him—and anything else he found had the prospect of being worse. "Let me think about it," he temporized.

"What's there to think?" she said. "You've got it down to a fine science. You don't have some foolish notion you're prostituting yourself?" She looked at him in amusement.

What could he say that she'd be willing to hear? That the job had been a stop-gap affair. That he was going stale with the repetition? That he had to give his energy to his own work. "Mildred," he said, "I've done twelve."

"So you want to bail out, eh? Sick of it—up to the gills with it, eh? Yeah, I've seen them, all the little boys and girls who want to do art. Do something original. Burn with a hard gemlike flame—I've even given a few of them house room." She gave a little sniff. "How many go on and do anything worth pissing on? Answer me. One in a thousand, when all's said and done— maybe one in ten thousand. I know—the rest have their go at it. They paint their little canvases and write their little plays and audition for acting jobs, and scribble out their passionate prose. And you know what? I was among them. Can you feature that? I even won prizes." For a moment she seemed to dip down into some memory of herself that brought her to a shrug and a small ironic dismissal.

She looked at him sharply. "And what do you think you've got that's so special? Even if you had the talent, you haven't got the moxie to..."

"Wait a minute," he said, blindsided by her attack. What was eating her? "I thought you liked what I was doing."

"Do you know how many are operating at that level of talent? Dozens. And not a drop more. No, you don't have it. And if you ever do, it'll surprise the hell out of both of us."

"So who the hell are you?"

"I'm trying to do you a favor," she said. "Save you some grief. Reputations are made in New York," she said. "How many have got what it takes to hack it there? You may as well paint still-lifes. It'll get you farther than anything else you've done."

It was all he could do to keep from hitting her. Only there was no arguing, no proof to offer. Only the nagging suspicion that she might be right. "Okay," he said. "I'll just do that."

"Twelve more," she said.

The next week he was fueled by some sort of fever that turned days and nights into one continuous reel of shifting images in his head—all with the intensity of the Spanish still life, but of a reality heightened beyond it. He hardly knew what he was doing. He called in sick, went to bed and slept and sweated for hours. When he woke, wrung out, thirsty beyond belief, he didn't know day from night. He went to the sink and poured water down his throat until he felt bloated and mopped his face. For a time he sat staring at his hand, as though it were a strange attachment for which he had not yet discovered the use. He felt an overwhelming urge to paint.

He seized a canvas he had primed and set it on the easel. From the wall where the model hung the orange bird hunched as though it were shivering in its feathers. He hardly glanced at it. He could have painted the whole thing from memory. He had grown into habit and laid in the colors he'd used a dozen times before. No sweat. Then as he surveyed the pulsating blobs of color on his palette, he was seized by something equivalent to the fever that had taken him before, and from that point on he painted like a man possessed.

Whatever object he shaped with his brush took on a life its form could hardly contain. From the grapes, a bursting fullness—within each a small universe exploding into being. The apples rolled from their position lethal with temptation as the lobster moved in, straight from the sea, in its claw a wriggling frog with a human face. Beneath his hand, the drape and backdrop turned to rocks and trees, an original garden writhing with copulating human and animal forms. Monkeys swung from the vines. He struggled for order amid the riot of color and movement. Before he collapsed altogether, the eye of the orange bird caught his and wouldn't release his gaze, as though they had made some sort of pact. It looked ready to take off for some other dimension.

He woke early, for the first time in days breathing easily. It took him a while to remember where he was or to collect any of the pieces of the previous days. He had no idea how long the fever had engulfed him. His head was cool, and he felt as though a sweet breeze was playing around him. He remembered he'd been painting. It was only six, he saw from his watch, of whatever day was dawning. He slipped on his clothes, stepped outside to breathe the air. Then he went back in, turned on the lights and stood in front of the painting. He couldn't believe it. Someone else had painted it, not himself at all—taking inspiration from some source that lay beyond him. Well, he thought. Well. For all its madcap flourishes, it seemed more real than anything he'd painted before.

When Mildred arrived at the gallery, he was ready for her. As she walked in the door, he stood naked but for a hastily devised loin cloth, his hair matted and falling into his face—holding up the painting.

It required a moment for her to take him in. "What is this, some kind of joke? Look, I've got things to do. Are you out of your mind or what?"

"Number thirteen," he said. "The lucky number." He danced around the room with it. "I changed a few things."

Suddenly there were monkeys everywhere, cavorting through the gallery, hanging from the fixtures, crapping on the floor, monkeys somersaulting, hanging by their tails. The orange bird had risen from immobility and was flapping around the room. He saw in the middle Mildred's face forming "The Scream," best painted by Munch, the clock melting down the wall, courtesy of Dali, the chair she stood in front of suddenly grabbing her and closing around her ankles, thanks to Remedios Varo. The copulating figures tumbled through the gallery, while the red and yellow flowers grew gigantic as cabbages. "Get out, get out," she yelled at him. Naked through the gallery he streaked, blowing her a kiss. Naked, into the alley, monkeys clamoring around him.

Exiles

H e's been through hell, Suz," Peter said. "Nothing original—just one more extension of the current hell we've
been creating for ourselves. The Albanian version—" Peter had
stopped by on the way to his house just up the road, ostensibly
to see how she was doing, but five minutes into the gin and tonic
she'd offered him Suzannah knew what was really on his mind.
He brought out a letter with foreign postage for her inspection,
and Suzannah considered a handwriting of broad clear strokes
and a row of foreign stamps, black on gray. "I don't know what's
coming off—I never know who's mucking around with power
these days. Things are so volatile there, one disruption after another. They're mostly crooks and spies, for all I can figure out."

The Spanish afternoon denied any trace of skullduggery,
but insisted vividly on pomegranate trees and ripening melons
in the extending fields. Geraniums and roses cast their reds and
pinks about the edges of the patio. "All the way up here I just
kept thinking about him. I'm afraid for him and Anna. Maybe we could get them out of the country for a while—at least
'til things cool off. I've been trying to convince them to go to
Paris."

He looked at her as one with ready sympathies, a fellow conspirator. "They can travel out of the country now, only none of them have any money." He shrugged, acknowledging the irony. "They have that freedom anyway." Peter, of course, would be footing the bill. He'd made it his life, taking up the cause of people on the run—persecuted writers and artists, people in every sort of political danger, even musicians down on their luck, actors out of work—sponsoring and befriending them. Indeed he'd been Suzannah's mainstay and support through all her own trouble—the merely personal. He gave her a kind of reassurance, his faith that certain things mattered, held firm in a world torn apart by ethnic conflicts and struggles for power, by bombs and money.

So here was the latest victim. From Eastern Europe, or Latin America, parts of Africa, they came, seeking his help and protection. A friend had told them of him or the friend of a friend. Peter provided an oasis, whatever money and connections could do. They were devoted to him—men and women, whatever their various races and tribes, religions and sects. She'd met a few—mostly Eastern Europeans, uprooted intellectuals, torn from their cultures, hoping for a way back after years of exile. And though there'd been some few along the way who'd borrowed what they never intended to return, or taken advantage of him in other ways, in one case turning on him viciously, none of it fazed him. He'd spent most of his inheritance on such humanitarian efforts, traveling behind the Iron Curtain before it fell, smuggling out manuscripts, letters and news, gathering up personal accounts, translating poems and stories, which he published in an obscure magazine in Geneva. Except for his sometimes neglected career as a sculptor, this was his life.

She guessed what was coming—he was trying to involve her in the drama—perhaps to take her mind off her own situation. Appealing to her own sense of exile and tentativeness. The question was still in her mind, whether to give up her house now that she had nothing to keep her in Andalusia, and go back to the States or just to sit there, a permanent visitor, and let life happen to her, as opposed to Peter, who was a citizen of the world.

"Has he been in prison?" she asked. An obligatory question. Being in prison, escaping from prison were constant threads of Peter's narratives.

He gave a wry smile. "No, by some miracle. He didn't do anything overtly antagonistic to the regime. The threat was always there—his wife and children were harassed as well. He never took up political issues in his novels, but there everything is political. Under the old regime, you couldn't say, 'There are no goods on the shelves,' without being considered subversive—I suppose that is a political statement. But now it sounds like he has a new set of spies to contend with. "

It always dismayed her to learn that one set of evils had been exchanged for another, that the hope of progress you tried to live with suffered so many detours.

"All those unreconstructed hardliners," he went on. "Those in power never let go without a struggle. They're still entrenched—"

Now there was a new danger. His friend had published a piece demanding that the files collected by former spies and informers be opened to the public. He'd roused a storm in political circles, even among other writers and artists. "But I think they're largely creatures of the new power structure," Peter said. "Not Karlo. He's a feisty sort, very intense—he never lets down. They couldn't intimidate him. The police called him in I don't know how many times. He didn't scare."

How dreadful it all was. Just when you thought the bastions had been stormed and some new light was being let into the cellars, you discovered the old rot was still there, giving off its fatal corruption. She didn't want any of it, didn't want to think about it. There were too many items in the news as it was: Rwanda, Kosovo, East Timor. Iraq, and always the various rumblings in the Middle East or India.

"He can stay with me as soon as I can get the repairs done, but you've seen how things are." A poplar tree had keeled over during a wind and damaged the roof and one of the bedrooms of the abandoned farmhouse Peter was rebuilding. The workmen would come when they could get to it. "It's just that—"

Yes, the situation was pressing. She couldn't refuse him, even ignoring that she was in his debt. After all, she was in the house alone—she had room to take in a whole family, if need be. Her sisters from the States had been to visit, but just now she was without company. "Let them come, by all means," she said, before a certain dismay set in. She would have to deal with these people, what they represented—their very presence would demand it. Deal with injustices she had no way of addressing, suffering she could hardly assuage. In some ways it might be a cruelty—offering them merely a respite from things she considered unimaginable and then throwing them back into it. Unless they simply fled. But even then— She would have to summon up suitable words as she took in her visitors, instead of sinking into her own inner space, as she did now, sometimes staring out over the garden until Elvira came to her in the fading light to tell her supper was on the table. Or else if she sat reading, she would suddenly rouse herself to discover the book had fallen open in her lap at some odd page, while her mind had wandered.

"Good—you'll like them," Peter said, getting up to leave, mission accomplished. "Like I say, Karlo's intense—almost too much so at times—I could tell you some stories. But there's such a warmth, such passion.... And his wife is lovely, very brave. She speaks English well."

Various phone calls during the next few days, and it was arranged, though not as they'd planned. Karlo was eager to come; his wife, who had an office job, would remain to look after things. Better not to have it look as though they were beating a retreat. Later perhaps— Suzannah's own concern with appearances was less dramatic. Wouldn't it seem awkward—that was her first response—to have an unattached male in the house? And cause comment? She was sensitive to conventions—she was, after all, a foreigner. As though sensing her hesitation, Peter offered assurance. "The workmen should be finishing up not long after we get back. I'll have my new studio then and invite everybody over."

First Peter would drive to Barcelona to pick Karlo up at the airport, and they would spend several days in the city before they appeared in the village. Meanwhile, she had Elvira prepare the guest room and primed herself to meet her visitor with a combination of sympathy and admiration: he'd done what she could never conceive of doing, lived at the edge where everything was at risk. She tried imagining life as a single breath, a single space of hazard. What sort of man was this—what had his experience done to him? She was unprepared to answer such a question for herself. By comparison, she seemed to have so little at stake. If it came to it, she wondered, what would she stand for? Could she claim any sort of courage? She doubted it. Nor did she have Peter's selflessness and dedication.

Her husband's business had created a world—she'd served it, had raised two children, now settled in their own careers in the States, had given her spare time as a volunteer to help teach English. That phase of her life over, she felt a certain relief—no more entertaining, no more tasteless jokes—but she had nothing to replace it. She knew herself only from the mirror, an uncertain image: a woman aging, without a clear future.

On the day of arrival, she was nervous, as though she were being put on trial. Elvira answered the door, and Peter brought him in. They were quite a pair—Peter: tall, big-boned, with a large head, broad freckled face and thick dark-red hair—who completely dwarfed his companion: small, slender, almost a head shorter than she herself. Yet he was an immediate presence. Proud nose, square jaw—sharply cut features. She was reminded of a hawk chick she'd once found in the road, which she'd approached tentatively to see if it was injured. It gave out a shriek that seemed to involve every cell of its body. All hawk—don't touch. Something to be reckoned with. And this, she thought, was Karlo. But when he smiled, she saw no bird of prey.

Indeed his face lit up when he saw her, and she read interest, eagerness. His smile was almost boyish, forget the shoddy dental work. "Very please I make your acquaintance." He took her palm in his. "To your house, which you so kindly offer, I offer the world's smallest writer," He added a grandiose gesture, inviting her to laugh at him. "My books, you pile them up, and they are higher than my head."

"You're boasting," Peter said. To Suzannah, he said, "Don't confuse this with humility—you'd be making a mistake."

"The world's smallest writer is welcome," she said.

His eyes sparkled. "I saw you before," he said. "when you didn't know."

"Me? Where?" she said, surprised, looking to Peter in her puzzlement.

"Peter and I walk on the beach this morning—he told me there is the lovely lady you stay with. Suzannah—if she had been Helen, she would launch a thousand ships. And now I see you."

"You see what a difference you made in the day," Peter said. "We waved, but you didn't notice. I didn't want to break into your reverie."

"Ah." She had indeed gone out that morning, walked along the beach as she often did, as if she could walk out her inner confusion, lose herself in the vistas of sand and sea—so self-absorbed in that state she didn't trouble to notice anything else. But she'd been seen—it made her feel strange, almost as if she'd been exposed, spied upon. She gave a little laugh to conceal her discomfort.

If he was enjoying a certain triumph at having caught her in a private moment, the softness of his look suggested that he found it precious. A romantic, she decided. Not at all shy. She'd come across them before. Gallantry above everything. A male thing—or maybe a European thing. To be lavished on any woman whatever her age. She grew skeptical before it. Entering foreign cultures had always intimidated her. All the things you could trip over, misinterpret. Americans blundered in like golden retriever pups, their innocence making a shambles.

Then it occurred to her a tone had been established that might offer both of them a cover. They could banter with each other, concealing more than they revealed, taking nothing seriously. Perhaps she had been given the key for getting through the next couple of days. She tried for some image of the spot in the Balkans he'd come from and what it might mean to be an Albanian. She knew something of Romania and Yugoslavia, but, for him, things had been pushed over another notch. What did it mean to come from the poorest, most isolated country in Europe? She couldn't quite take him in, though he and Peter seemed to have the ease of an established friendship, two men not too far apart in age—Karlo looked to be in his mid-fifties; Peter, somewhat older. Peter brought in his bags, and they got him settled in his room. She explained how the shower in the adjoining bath operated.

Afterward in the living room, a glass of sangria in hand, Karlo looked edified, almost glowing. "Let me know if there is anything you need," she said. She'd invited Peter to stay for dinner—Elvira had prepared paella, and for the first time since Warren's death, the meal was served in the dining room with its handsome carved furniture. Karlo looked around appreciatively. "Very beautiful," he said, his gesture taking in wood and tile and brightly decorated plates along the walls. "I can tell you love things that are beautiful."

The tone was genuine, the words carrying a kind of recognition that gave her a little burst of pleasure. After their initial argument, Warren had left the decoration of the house entirely to her. Whereas he'd have torn out everything, modernized the old farmhouse with the most expensive fixtures money could buy, she'd found craftsmen to restore old walls and tile work, to redo the floors. She'd searched in the city for furniture and tiles and found a gardener to put in plants and flowers. There was something more than pleasure in all of it, as though she were reentering a former life, bringing it to consciousness. In the end Warren had been won to something like enthusiasm, especially when his associates looked around and said, "Nice place you've got here."

She tried to ask Karlo about his work. "Later, I will explain," he said, "I will give you my life."

Oh dear, she thought. When she went to bed that night, she was exhausted, yet all keyed up. She slept restlessly.

When they met in the morning for breakfast, Karlo was full of energy. Already he'd gone for a walk, and seemed more at home almost than she. Elvira served them *café con leche*, brought them hard-boiled eggs, a plate of cheese and ham and toast with butter and jam. "How good you are to have me here," he said, palms extended. "I wake in palace like the Arabian nights."

"It's a pretty modest palace," she said, smiling. "I'm sorry your wife couldn't come."

"Yes. Better for us both. She can speak the English. I can only...." His hands moved into the space where vocabulary failed him.

But he could look at her. Whenever they came together, his expression made a place only for her, his gaze intent but receptive, as though to see her in pristine clarity. It made her feel as she had when he told her he'd seen her without her knowing. Perhaps the absence of language brought into play something more basic or primitive, more observant and receptive. More passionate. Was that the word? She hesitated before it, there was such immediacy in the notion. As though his eyes were open, informed by some vision that he alone had access to. She had no idea what he saw—would have been glad to stand back from herself and see it too. Maybe it wasn't there at all. For herself, she found it difficult to form a clear picture of him, grasp a sense of his experience beyond what Peter had told her. A film, a scrim seemed to lie between his image and her eyes. She sensed a deficiency. She could only add up the daily facts of his presence.

The work at Peter's was going more slowly than expected. A lot of his roof had to be reconstructed. Materials hadn't come. Various delays. She was relieved that in the days that followed Karlo actually made few demands on her. The routine of the household went undisturbed. Most mornings he was up early and after a walk on the beach and their meeting for breakfast, he went to his room or set up a card table in the garden to work. He was intent on finishing the draft of a novella he had brought to Spain to work on. Whenever she glanced out at him, she found him frowning with concentration. Sometimes he worked all day. Sometimes he stayed up 'til all hours like some night animal tracking its prey. How intense the impulse that carried him—she envied him.

But if he came to a momentary block, Peter was there on his motorcycle to whisk him off. Quite a picture, the two of them. Karlo would mount on the back, clasping Peter around the waist, and off they roared to the beach, to the surrounding towns. She loved to watch them take off. A motorcycle—somehow it was fitting.

She tried to negotiate a state of affairs where her visitor could do as he pleased without feeling ignored. As the days passed, she felt she should rouse herself from her torpor—do something for him. "He must be bored...," she started to say to Peter.

"On the contrary, for him, boredom would be self-indulgence. He has all he needs."

She felt rebuffed. "I just thought he'd like to meet some other people," she countered. "A dinner party—"

"Of course," Peter said. "I was just trying to reassure you..."

They went ahead with the plan, bringing together those who formed what might be called their society, a combination of Spaniards and expatriates. The Porters and the Welds, British couples who'd retired there to escape the climate at home were on hand, an American couple on a Fulbright, as well as a French painter Peter knew, who had come for the summer, a couple of Spanish journalists down from Madrid for the weekend, the owner of a local bookshop, a German winegrower Warren had cultivated, and a Bosnian translator who had left the country during the civil wars.

It was more than she'd bargained for. After the usual introductory chitchat and the first glass of sangria, the hubbub began to drown out the single voices, but over at the edge the conversation grew increasingly declamatory. The Americans were embittered over the way politics was creating a witch hunt at home. But what had Spain been through? the journalists reminded them. The rest of Europe? The Bosnian was eager to blame the Europeans and the Americans for the state of things in the Balkans. The shelling of Dubrovnik—that's when they should have stepped in. "You think only of yourselves," the Bosnian said. "You are drunk with your ideal of goodness. You play with triviality while the world falls into ruins. Democracy!" He could have spat.

Karlo leapt in. "You think the Iron Curtain is gone, everything is clean as rain. Only look—corruption, corruption everywhere. You have heard the pyramid scheme—everybody loses their money." He explained in detail. "You cannot imagine—it is like a hell. Underground—people tearing each other—like sharks."

She'd been standing with the Porters, who'd been trying to hold onto the notion of a friendly gathering. "You've got to start out with solid institutions," Bryan Porter said leaning over to Suzannah, as though revealing a secret. As in India, she thought. She caught the cigar smoke on his breath. "Otherwise, you're just done for, aren't you?" He sent his hand in a downward plunge.

"I don't want to think about politics anymore," his wife, Gwyneth, said on the other side of her. "It gives me a headache." She was a small woman with watery blue eyes and blonde hair turning toward gray. "I just want my *Guardian*, my good English marmalade, and a little dancing now and then. That's not much to ask, is it?"

"No, dovey," her husband said, "though I could do without the dancing."

She gave him a little punch, and looked at Suzannah, as though to draw her into being amused. She was trying to help.

"Now a group of informers, out of the old ones," Karlo went on, gathering momentum, gesticulating wildly. "They can't stop being what they are. Like scorpions—they cannot help being scorpions. There is a secret file on me, others—"

People looking at you with hostile intent—and how, Suzannah wondered, could you maintain your innocence in that? No one was invisible. No, there were always eyes on you.

"Oh dear," Gwyneth murmured as she sipped her drink. "Having to be like one of those little feisty dogs, all so worked up."

"And with very sharp teeth," Suzannah said. Something like acid scalded her mouth, and she had to excuse herself. If only one could take refuge— In what? Not innocence certainly. She refilled her wine glass. An old ploy. Wine made her rosy and voluble, excited her into being charming.

"How can we live—if we don't purge away these evil things?" It was becoming a drama—he was forcing people to listen to him in spite of themselves. "Why the files should be open? Otherwise, I tell you, the future is poisoned. What are we, the writers, the intellectuals?—not cunning like spies. No, we forgive the wound and do not ask revenge. Otherwise how can we live?"

His plaint ran like a litany in her head, as she went off to the kitchen to tell Elvira to serve the food. Perhaps it would bring a little calm.

If there was something to live for... The smell of food assured her that there was. It was beginning to make inroads into the consciousness of the guests. Or perhaps the discussion had reached one of those peaks at which, for the moment, there was a necessary pause. At any rate, there was a movement toward the table as soon as Elvira and her daughter, Beatrice, set out the platters of paella with its rich combination of seafood, chicken, sausage and rice. They brought platters of fresh tomatoes and avocados, baskets of bread. Politics dissipated into the homey and personal. Gwyneth asked Suzannah how her sister was, and Peter wanted to know if the Porters were organizing a trip this year to Lorca for the bullfights. "Lorca?" Karlo pricked up his ears. "Look, I carry him in my pocket. He is the prince—my poet. Just like Alexander with *The Iliad*."

Gwyneth smiled, puzzled, then moved past distraction, "Of course—it's the great event. We're dying to see 'El Cordobes.'"

"You enjoy the slaughter?" Karlo said. "You don't have enough?"

"It's a great art," the Porters insisted.

"And my Lorca, yes, he loved them."

"You must see a bullfight while you're in Spain."

"For the cruelty?"

"For brilliance and daring."

Afterward, little conversations sprang up in various parts of the living room at the edge of a central bonfire that roared on

until, finally, after the others had departed, Karlo was left with
Peter and the two Spanish journalists, who raked over the state
of things in the Balkans, speculated about the future of Kosovo
and what Karlo would be going home to, if he did go back. This
group finally broke up around two in the morning. Peter apologized to Suzannah for keeping her up so late. After Peter left,
Karlo poured himself another drink and paced up and down,
apparently replaying what had gone on before. "Goodnight,"
she said.

He looked up, came to himself. "Oh, I am sorry. Please forgive me—always I am carried away. You will not get your sleep."
He came to her and took her hand. "Thank you," he said. "You
did this for me—I am grateful for all you do."

When you were poor, you became rich in gratitude. She had
learned that much in her various travels in the world.

Had Warren ever been that poor? Suzannah wondered. She
was keyed up herself, as though she had just witnessed a gun
battle.

When her husband was killed in an air crash leaving Sin-
gapore, her sisters, as well as her children, tried to persuade
Suzannah to come back home to the States as soon as possible.
Why would she, a woman alone, want to stay in Spain? Her
older sister, Margot, came over for almost two weeks to help
Suzannah through this period of loss and confusion, though
Suzannah suspected that Margot very likely thought her better off. It had been a difficult marriage. For all his success in
the overseas management of a consulting firm, he seemed per-
petually angry that his singlemindedness had landed him only
the number two spot in the firm. His rage shaped a family life
in which he bullied Suzannah and sons into some version of
perfection that kept changing—or else he ignored them. Away
for months at a time trying to win contracts for his company's
services, he took an annual holiday reluctantly so that Suzannah
and the kids could reconnect with their relatives in Connecticut. His own parents were dead, and he avoided his sister, who

was habitually short of cash. Earlier in his career, his job had taken him to Indonesia, Yugoslavia, and Romania.

Margot had tried Bali and Belgrade, but Bucharest had been too much for her. Spain, she decided, was far more civilized. She couldn't fault the beaches of Andalusia and the chance to sunbathe. But after two weeks she was glad enough to get back to the familiar environment of New Britain. "Now you must put yourself together and go on with your life," she insisted. "You're still an attractive woman. And you know Gordon Mason—he still asks me about you. He's doing well in that pharmacy— he runs it now."

"Aren't you getting a little ahead of the game?" Suzannah protested. "As if my first thought was another man. How can you? I know you didn't like Warren…." She burst into tears.

"Oh, Suzy," Margot said, putting her arms around her. "I just want you to be happy for once—"

"And what makes you think," Suzannah said, drawing back, "that I wasn't happy?" Her face was hot.

Margot looked at her in dismay. "Oh dear," she murmured. "But at least consider the house," she said. "I know it's a hard time for you to be practical-minded. It's so big," she said, holding out her hands, looking around her. "You'll rattle around in it like a pebble. And who are you going to keep company with—yes, I know, you've introduced me to the Porters and that woman with the wart on her lip. But you know how it is with a single woman. All the married women think she's after their mates and . . . "

"Please, Margot," she said, "This is the life we built here, Warren and I. You wouldn't have chosen it, but…"

"So I ought to mind my own business—indeed I should," she said. "You were always the one who wanted to go your own way, and if that's what you want…"

"I don't know what I want," Suzannah cried. "How can I know—here, now?"

"I just thought you might need a refuge. We're there." She offered herself, the rest of the family, with open palms.

A sudden image of them all with open arms amused her. And beyond the prickly surface of Margot's affection was something she could count on. "I know—"

Though she was glad her sister had come, bringing the feel of the air she had breathed in the past, a sense of continuity, her own unresolved state made another presence a distraction, if not an irritant. She was hardly reluctant to see her go. Just as she was relieved to get past the visits of condolence from people she scarcely knew, the messages she had to answer. "Your husband was a man of utmost integrity and large ideas. He pushed himself to the limit." Indeed. His titanic energy had exhausted her. At times she wondered if he'd enjoyed his life.

When she'd done what was required, signed the necessary papers for the lawyer and accountant, worked past the bureaucratic snarls, and was now waiting for the accountant to settle matters of taxes and inheritance, the house loomed large and empty and quiet. She had wanted to be alone. She was reminded, though, hearing Elvira, their cook, and Beatrice, who kept the house spotless, laughing and gossiping in the kitchen, that she was a stranger here. Even though Suzannah spoke Spanish fluently now, there lay that zone where sound subsided into silence, and she was teased by a music half heard, by a space around and beyond words, shimmering with implications. Some inchoate possibility or nuance that beckoned, only to elude her.

Into that mood now Karlo had stepped. And though, like her sisters, he had always lived in the same place, where his writing made him truly a part of the culture, it struck her as they talked that he was as much an exile as she. A kind of spokesman for those who suffered and yearned in silence, still he was caught in the net of lies and intrigues that shaped the common anguish.

"You look around,"—his eyes darting furtively—"you don't know who are your friends. Some artists, writers now they are mad at me for what I write."

At least he was led by some deep unswerving impulse. In the light of his, her own loneliness seemed a pallid affair. Simply a series of moves from one place to another occasioned by her husband's work. Just when she'd got settled in a place, found connections, a common bond among those similarly situated, she'd had to pick up and move somewhere else, saying goodbye to friends from Australia or Britain or Germany or Japan, with whom she'd exchange Christmas letters, but seldom, if ever, see again.

She'd felt oddly shaped by Warren's business, his motive for being there his only real focus—that left the real life of the place untouched. Meanwhile she'd had to carve out some sort of life for them—find schools for Nancy and Edward, do volunteer work with agencies that worked among the poor, socialize mostly with Warren's associates. Her role. For his part, he kept them in comfortable quarters, found servants to look after the cooking, clean the apartment, tend the garden. There was a car and driver to take them to markets and schools and clinics, to restaurants and gatherings. She'd hired tutors, tried to learn the language she heard in the street, now, it seemed, a garbled language of many tongues. That sense of ever keeping an ear cocked without fully understanding had given her a sense of how dependent she was on the good will of even the least of those who washed her clothes or prepared her food, as she pretended all the while she was fully in charge. An odd play of mutual preservation they enacted, she and her servants, who wanted only to cling to their good positions and not be sent away. Their mingled insecurities bred a curious sort of loyalty in those who loved her, a barely concealed contempt in those who could only see her game. She'd survived, however, with her life a bricolage taken from the various cultures she'd been exposed to.

The oasis was those few weeks in Connecticut with her sisters and nieces and nephews. Family. A life that seemed more solid, more meaningful than her own, with her children in international schools, finally going off to college in the States. There lay continuity, stability—a certain desirable boredom. The family had been in the town since the post-Civil War era, rooted there.

So that what happened now surprised her, her resistance to go back to all that she'd missed over the years. "Really, Suzy," Margot wrote as the weeks lengthened into months, "I don't understand you at all. All those years you've never had a home and couldn't wait until you were back on native soil…. And Jim has married such a delightful girl."

Poor thing, they thought of her—having to keep uproot-ing herself and the kids, starting all over again. Yet despite all the years of looking at herself through their eyes, what surfaced again after those coveted visits was that she was no longer of the common mind. She'd stepped beyond the mold that shaped her earlier life and would feel almost as much an outsider if she moved back.

Foreign speech with its varying accents, the richness of skin colors, the differences of atmosphere and orientation, the smells of different food cooking—these were the stimuli she responded to now and she found a curious reassurance in them. She missed a certain innocence and energy she found back home, but its trivializing influence, its bumbling self-assertion put her off. To whom could she speak? Those friendships that had formed out of the sense of the temporary were particularly intense. Giv-en their common condition, their ethos of the temporary, her friends opened their lives to her, and, in effect, became her fam-ily. She felt she'd left some part of herself in each of the places she'd lived. Perhaps if she could retrieve all these fragments and put them together, she sometimes thought, with more hope than conviction, they would yield a whole greater than the sum of its parts.

She had been making herself sort through the boxes of stuff that had moved with them over the years and had sat gathering time in the closets. Things she'd forgotten. Correspondence and papers she burned in the fireplace; clothes she would distribute among various charities, wondering now why she'd kept them. Old treasures the kids had given her—these she put aside. She found an odd assortment of things—some shadow puppets she'd never unpacked and a tiger carved from teak.

Then a box with her old paints and drawing things and a sheaf of her various attempts. She'd carried them with her over the years, always knowing they were there, but leaving them aside. She brought out a little painting of Warren she'd done not long after they were married. What a struggle to get him to

sit still for her. She smiled as she contemplated the youthful features. Not bad, she thought. She'd caught a certain expression,
a kind of constant that had traveled down the years of aging
features—both proud, with a touch of arrogance, and defensive.
Next a drawing of their old cat, Sunny. A striped yellow cat
they'd had to leave behind with her mother when Warren took
his first job abroad. She couldn't tell whether he remembered
her on their visits home. There were a few landscapes, unfin-
ished drawings mostly—a couple of her better efforts from high
school. She'd never thought of herself as painting seriously; yet
she'd held onto these early efforts. She'd even taken an art class
during one of their sabbaticals in the States and for a while she'd
been stirred by an intention. She discovered a little sketchbook
she'd carried for a while, recording rice fields in Bali and some
willows along a river in Romania. She'd meant to do something
with them. But there had been too many distractions—she'd
found it hard to carve out a solitary space, to make room for
herself. She lifted out a box of pastels she'd bought in Hartford,
barely used, and a box of water colors, a pad of paper.

She sorted through the brushes, found an old favorite and
smoothed out the hair. She looked over the tin of paints, red and
yellow, orange and blue, and felt an old excitement. She went for
a glass of water, then looked around for subject matter—something simple. Fruit. From the bowl on the dining room table she
selected two pomegranates and three green figs and arranged
them on a white plate bordered with a blue and yellow design.
She studied the arrangement for a moment, moved one here,
adjusted another there. The red and green cast their juxtaposed
reflections on the plate. Yet to try to capture the effect seemed
quite beyond her. Tentatively she put down a wash, laid in another, then found herself growing intent upon what she was
doing, forgetting everything. After she'd laid in the washes, she
took up a pencil for some line, deepened the colors. Gradually
the painting emerged.

"Ah, you paint," Karlo said, coming up behind her. She
hadn't heard him approach.

"Oh hardly," she said, flustered, caught again. "I just..."
But she had no desire to explain.

"Of course, I knew it," he said, as though he'd made an important discovery. "Art is truth and beauty—"

"Oh," she said, "I'm just doing a little water color." It was too much to stand before truth and beauty, even if they came only with small letters. Hastily she closed up her paints.

Since Karlo's arrival, she had the sense that time and motion had shifted from a gray stillness into a rapid current, set in motion by Karlo's intense preoccupations. Disoriented, she wanted to stay where she was, keep the future at bay. Yet when she turned away, it was to a fading past. She tried to extract something hard and firm to take to the present moment, but her recollections seemed part of another landscape. With Warren she had shared a life. But even the remnants of grief couldn't sustain it, offer proof of her experience. She lacked further imagination.

But Karlo seemed a free agent—a presence, whether he was working on his novella or roaring off with Peter. Perhaps he was simply enjoying himself, unaware of the challenge he offered her. (Damn the unpredictability of workmen, who had conspired to set him so emphatically in her midst. Peter was all apology, but what could he do?) Karlo was grounded in purpose, she was adrift. She yearned to reclaim her space, not to have to answer to anybody. Yet who did she have to answer to? But the prospect of being alone, rattling around in the house, as Margot put it, daunted her as well.

She tried to stand back, decently attentive as a hostess, but at the same time a woman who had her own concerns. The phone still rang constantly—something from lawyer, accountant, Warren's firm, various businesses, family, friends and acquaintances. She made herself go out for lunch or coffee with this one and that. These occasions left her with a sense of dissipated energy. On the other hand, Peter seemed determined to have her join their adventures. More and more they were a threesome.

Indeed the day at Agua Amargo was a gift. Peter knew the place from his various wanderings around Andalusia, but it had been a while since he'd been there. Though he was certain they'd prostrate themselves at his feet in gratitude for his taking them there, he was, he told them, killing two birds with one stone. First there was the wonderful sandy beach. They could swim and lie out in the sun. And there was a taverna where they could have lunch. But for him, it was the stuff he could scavenge on the beach. The treasures—what he could turn up for his sculptures. It was a particularly good beach for that. Suzannah marveled at what he could do with bits of driftwood and bone, with feathers and shards of glass, even pieces of old tire, plastic cups, bits of metal and rusted wire, dented beer cans. The stuff you kicked aside in disgust—unless, of course, you were Peter—or a child. If only you could go back to a six-year-old's intensity.... His studio was a little museum of odds and ends that he'd reclaimed, waiting for their translation into forms that Suzannah found sometimes whimsical, sometimes formidable, like forgotten icons.

They arrived at a little cove framed by hills falling away to shelves of rock and stony outcroppings. To one side was a sandy beach, quiet perfect for swimming. And how inviting it was, the water pale green and gold with the sun on it, sliding over colored stones. The rest of the beach was scattered with such stones, and rocks and shells and bunches of seaweed. "Perfect," Peter said. "We've got the place to ourselves. Just look at the colors." As though they'd all been hit by the same impulse, the three of them were one, each moving along, bending, picking up stones or shells, examining them, showing them off. "If you find a pure round one, white... but translucent," Karlo said, "I will trade for this beautiful.... Look, it has a landscape on it." "What can this be—I've never seen a green like it. It can't be natural—and the shape." "It's a piece of tile," Peter said. "I can use it, if you don't want it." "By all means."

Suzannah looked back at their prints in the sand. Kids, she thought. Or maybe just idiots, the sun beating on their heads, turning their brains into mercury and salt. It was hot, she was sweating. She bounded over the hot sand, dumped her treasures next to her towel and ran down the beach into the water. "Oh," she cried, it was so wonderfully cold. She waved to the others.

"You're crazy not to be in here," she yelled and plunged in. She swam out until she was breathless—out and farther out. Then she turned onto her back and floated with the waves, her eyes closed, giving herself to the lulling movement. How lovely. A wave dashed her.

She swam back in until she could put her feet down on a tussocky spot. She couldn't see Peter, but Karlo was swimming toward her. He tried to stand near her but he was beyond his depth. "So you tempt me," he said. "You think you're special because you have your rock." He tried to push her off. A struggle—he was much stronger than she expected. But just at the point of conquering, he dove down into the water, came up a little farther out, shaking water from his head and laughing. "This is Karlo's rock," he boasted. "The rock he rules. His kingdom."

They got out of the water together. "Where's Peter?" She didn't see him anywhere. He must have gone somewhere beyond the point.

"He will wander for miles," Karlo said, "until sundown—past hunger and thirst. He will forget us entirely, forget everything except popsicle sticks and pieces of plastic. Meanwhile we will starve."

"Yes," she agreed. The two men, she thought, understood one another.

Peter returned, full of enthusiasm, as they were drying off. Not only had he found inspiring bits of flotsam, but a pair of earrings someone must have laid on the sand when she went in to swim. It would be a sacrifice, but he would give them to Suzannah. "How lovely," she said, admiring the earrings, silver with little figures set with red stones.

"Now I must find you a treasure," Karlo said. "Maybe not now, here in this moment. But I will find one."

As though they were in some sort of competition. "What tribute," she said. A male thing, she supposed. Never outgrown. How laced with ironies. Peter hadn't the slightest interest in her. Somewhere in the past there'd been a rocky marriage, and afterward, from the oblique references he sometimes made, some short-lived affairs. Women loved him, but she suspected darker regions of temperament. Now he seemed interested mainly in what he found on the beach or what was thrown up on the tide of political absurdity. Only Karlo was caught up in some momentary fantasy. She wondered what his wife was like.

"Look at this." Peter called their attention to the skull and vertebrae from some small animal he'd found. "I might have done something with the earrings," he said, "but bones are more useful. And just look at this piece of root. Wonderful shape."

Karlo rubbed his belly. "I appreciate you have a great talent and you're now exploding with ideas…"

"We're starved," Suzannah said.

"In that case…" Peter said, and led them in the direction of the taverna.

There a young Italian woman remembered Peter, welcomed his friends, and at his request, showed them the kinds of fish that had been brought in that day that she could prepare. They chose a large fish with firm white meat that would feed the three of them, then sat down at a table under vine leaves in a little space of shade in the dazzling afternoon. They ordered a bottle of wine, exchanged toasts, attacked the bread and then the salad brought to them, and waited, teased by the odors of the cooking fish. Suzannah had never been so hungry.

The fish, the wine, the afternoon—the time went in a single rush of pleasure the three of them were reluctant to let go of. They drank a second bottle of wine and ordered a third. "I could stay here forever," Karlo said.

"I hope you will," Peter responded. "What's the news from home?"

Karlo shook his head. "Yet when I think of Tirane—it is such a beautiful place." They reminisced about Peter's visits to Albania. Karlo dramatized how he'd once outwitted some petty official by mimicking a superior and ordering him to give Karlo a permit and funds to attend a writers' meeting in Belgrade. Through Karlo's imitation, the official came across as particularly dense. The afternoon ended in great hilarity, and Suzannah yielded to their entreaties to go with them to Granada the next

day to visit the Alhambra. She had planned to go to Madrid—
she had business there. But it didn't seem pressing.

It turned out to be a peculiar day. They were late getting
started, waiting for Karlo, who appeared in suit and tie and
smelled of aftershave. "You've been all that time primping?"
Peter said. "You're expecting an audience with the last of the
Moorish kings?"

"I always hear about the Alhambra," Karlo said, as if he
could not fail to live up to the occasion. "The name of God written 9,000 times in one room alone."

All during the drive, he was pointing things out, as though
to preserve each thing in its special quality. The stray dog on the
road, the flock of sheep moving into the hills, certain trunks of
the olive trees, as they rayed into vastness over the hills. He was
exhausting.

A long drive to Granada and there it was, the walls of the
great palace overlooking the old section of the city below. They
bought their tickets, signed up to enter at one o'clock and were
on their way to a spot where they could eat the sandwiches
they had bought when Peter let out a yell and turned sharply,
"Ladron! Thief," and took out after a man shouldering his way
through the crowd. Other people started shouting. Karlo and
Suzannah tried to follow, but their path was blocked, and it was
impossible to see. A struggle apparently. Then the police. An
increasing crowd pressed around. They'd grabbed the man, and
Peter emerged with his wallet. He had to go the police station,
however. No, they shouldn't wait for him. He could see the Alhambra again anytime.

So she and Karlo gave themselves to the porticoes that
looked like lace in stone, admired the efflorescent color and design, the pools and fountains, the pavilion of lions, the gardens.
A marvel, all of it. And how splendid to walk there, two ordinary people in a place that had been stripped of its history. A
seat of power once, lost by a man more taken up with a woman
than with the threat of extinction. "A dangerous illusion—power," Karlo said. "You think it belongs to you. Somewhere in the
universe you listen and there is laughter."

She and Karlo spent a good deal of time in the gardens, with their exquisite roses, all colors and scents. Suzannah leaned over to smell them. Karlo did his own scouting, calling her to this one and that. After they'd made their way to the Generalife and then to the exit, Karlo pulled out from the inside of his coat the rose, a mixture of pink and yellow, they had found the most alluring and presented it to her. "For you." The promised offering. She had worn Peter's earrings.

"You can get into trouble for things like that," she said.

"What is there but trouble? It depends on the kind you want."

The next morning when she sat down to breakfast, she found a piece of paper on her plate with a verse printed out:

Why was I born between mirrors?
Day reflects me
and night copies me
in all its stars.

"Lorca," Karlo said, as he reached for a piece of melon.

What splendid egotism! That was him all over—to be part of the atmosphere, part of the air she breathed.

The following day the sheet printed with large generous strokes was on the table on the terrace, where she usually sat in the afternoon.

Free me from the martyrdom
of seeing myself without fruitage.

A knife went through her. Had he chosen words for her? And then another slipped under the door of her bedroom:

With a cape of wind
my love flung itself to the waves.

He wasn't at breakfast the next morning. He had business with Peter in town, Elvira told her, but he had left the book of poems beside her plate. "Read some Lorca today," he had written across a scrap of paper. Perhaps, she thought, she could find a verse that would protect her like a sword stroke.

But she wasn't called upon to marshall her defenses. The game, the contest, whatever it was—was shunted aside. For some days a sense of distraction caught at them, something immanent in the air, like static. The situation at home did not bode well. One of the factions had succeeded in creating havoc in the congress, and the political situation was close to anarchy. "The lies and callousness," Karlo raged. "More arrests and human rights violations. And what will that solve?"

He and Peter had long debates about which faction would win out, whether or not he should stay in Spain and send for Anna, what would happen if he went back. They could take temporary refuge there, Peter argued, with an eye to Paris, that refuge of expatriates, or even the States. Then after several days of brooding, of moods that ran from outrage to despair, Karlo appeared, looking as haggard as if he'd spent a month on a binge. "Pardon me for my very bad temper these past days," he apologized to Suzannah as he sat down with her for breakfast. "I have been terrible company—a great impose—how do you say?—on my hostess."

She tried to reassure him—but he waved her off. "No, inexcusable to make you a party of my part." He took a sip of coffee, sat silent for a moment. "Everything strikes here," he said, as he struck his chest. "But no more of it." He pushed it all aside. "I made up my mind. Yes, finally Karlo has to do that—stop making an ass of himself. It's about time. These past days— like a nightmare. Anyway," he announced, looking at her with haunted eyes, "I am going back. I will call Peter to arrange for the ticket."

He spoke as if it were his only choice. She felt a sudden chill, could almost have wept.

"You're surprised? Maybe I am too. But who would speak for them? These times—maybe they will be worse before they get better." He shrugged. "If I don't go back, I betray something—it is where I live, what my life has been. My experience, their experience—it's the same. That's where my books came from. Without them, what they have given me, what would I write? There are those who trust me."

She envied him. She no longer trusted even herself. At times her sense of reality seemed like foam disappearing into sand.

Karlo belonged somewhere, at least on his own terms. And when he left, she'd be back where she was before. The thought left her reeling.

The rest of their breakfast was taken up with small details, questions of what could be arranged. After breakfast he called Peter. Though Peter was surprised, concerned for him, he understood immediately and set about arranging things. Karlo would be able to leave the end of the week. Though he went back to work on his novella, a tension hung in the air. The day reflected him all right—all his moods, all his unpredictability.

"What I am in this kind of world is all right—nothing to lose. It comes down to myself—what I am."

"But aren't you afraid sometimes?" she asked him.

He looked at her. "And you're not?"

"And you've just told Gwyneth you'd go to the bullfights. Right after—"

"Even when I speak of the slaughter, the cruelty. But I must understand—I must see what Lorca saw, the deep emotion he discovered, that lives in his poetry. I must know that. I have come to this land of Spain and I will see what is here and if it is the same as what I know already. Perhaps I will discover. And you will come with me?"

It was more than a request. "I don't know," she demurred. "The blood—I'm afraid it will make me sick."

"Yes," he sympathized. "In the newspapers you don't have to look at it."

It was difficult to imagine the Porters as bullfight enthusiasts, but they made their trip to Lorca an annual pilgrimage. "It's the whole drama," Gwyneth said. "Putting their lives on the line just for those few moments in the ring. Absolutely thrilling, the courage of it."

"And the art," Bryan said. "It's such an art. Right now the bulls are at their prime—we'll see the real fighters."

Peter was less than enthusiastic. "Cruelty raised to an art," he said.

"Look, old fellow, that's all those bulls are good for. Most of them end up as beef anyway—except for the really fierce ones—the toros bravos. Very selective. For them it's a pampered life for four or five years. And then the final moment of glory. What more can you ask?"

"How about a willing cow and a little spot of flowery meadow," Suzannah suggested, as she adjusted her straw hat.

"A slaughter for public entertainment," Peter said. "What's the moment of truth these days?"

"Come now," Gwyneth said, as she directed them to the cars. "It's the heart of Spain—Flamenco and bullfights—you can't have one without the other."

"Ritual," Bryan contended. "Probably goes back to the bull sacrifices in Crete."

"Once they sacrificed human beings," Peter said. "Young girls, children. Now it's murder."

"Maybe that's why they call it war," Karlo said. "So they can do it anyway—without ceremony."

"Come on, you killjoys," Gwyneth said. They distributed themselves among the various cars. Suzannah tried to avoid the Porters' vehicle because Bryan was such an erratic driver, with sudden starts and lurches that made you grateful for seat belts; but they insisted she go with them. Peter drove off with Karlo while Bryan loaded the trunk with a chest of cold drinks and the food they'd packed for the occasion. They'd also brought pillows to sit on.

Tickets in hand, they entered into the babble of voices inside the arena and found their seats in the sun. Foolish to buy seats in the shade, the Porters commented. Before it was over all the seats would be in shade anyway. They watched the Spanish women make their entrances in their brilliant dresses, red, pink, yellow, with white ruffled sleeves and ruffled skirts. In the stands beside their men they were like exotic birds. The atmosphere was festive, expectant, the sun blazing. Then music to stir the blood. The grand entrance. First the officials, then the players in the drama—the picadors on horseback, the bandilleros, the matadors, all in their costumes.

Actors in place, the chute opened and the first bull came pounding into the arena, entering a strange space and a new experience. A force meeting an uncertainty. Suzannah stole a glance at Karlo next to her, his eyes riveted on the bull. Her breath caught. Peter had told her the bulls now were smaller, bred down for the bullfighters. Even so, it was more than enough. The sheer dark force of it, the horns that could gore and kill, the great head, the dewlap. It could still force its way into the mind with a single dizzying impression— You could still imagine a god rising out of it, out of nature and taking its form. A tension flowed through the crowd as one of the bandilleros ran the cape across the ground and the bull charged after it. Did it favor the left horn or the right? How would it charge? That was what you had to watch for.

Behind her Bryan was handing round bottles of beer and soft drinks and, gratefully, Suzannah took a lemonade. It was hot now—Karlo had shaped a hat out of a newspaper to shield himself from the sun. Gwyneth handed round the chicken sandwiches she had prepared. Suzannah held one in her hand, not sure if she could eat it. They were watching the picadors on their blindfolded horses stab the bull with their pointed spears. The bull lunged at one of the horses, throwing the picador to the ground. A gasp from the crowd as the others tried to lure the bull away and get the man to safety. Her stomach was a knot.

Now the two central figures of the drama emerged, matador and bull. All thought suspended, she entered into the dance between them, the series of veronicas made of charging bull and shifting cape. The excitement of the crowd was a palpable thing, the shouts of olé, with each skillful pass, the closeness of the horns. She almost forgot to breathe. And how expertly the bandilleros cast the sharp decorated sticks into the vulnerable spots to fire things up for the final encounter. Now with the muleta, the sword concealed underneath.

The moment seemed to break apart and she was spiraling inside it. The man had known from the outset what he faced, but the bull had to awaken to its fate and saw now the instrument of it, saw and would throw himself at it, trample it to the ground, if he could. As if in that moment of pure ferocity, in the recognition of the force that shaped its death, it too attempted to shape a death for what threatened, the process moving beyond the bull itself to something almost human. In the same moment, the eye and consciousness of the man were connected to the two eyes of the bull, both looking at the death that hovered over them. The passes very close to the horns now caught them in the deepest intimacy, as if only they existed, the spectators in the stands melting into illusion. Intimate as lovers, seeing nothing but each other, the flash of the cape, the maddened rush toward it, each knowing the other beyond all knowledge.

"Truly, this is art," Bryan Porter breathed behind her.

But she was dizzyingly caught up in what she had always known but never knew before. If anyone had so much as touched her the atoms of her being would have shot out in all directions.

Then the thrust of the sword, the gush of blood, the staggering animal. The bull came crashing to the ground, as the crowd went wild with applause; flowers rained from the stands. But for Suzannah came an overwhelming rush of disgust as the victorious torero received the ears and tail. She sat staring at the half ton of carcass being dragged from the arena and couldn't breathe. She wanted to get up and go outside and see no more, but there were five more bulls to watch.

Afterward she could scarcely remember any but the first contest. She didn't know what she felt about it, couldn't find any suitable words. She barely listened to what the others were saying on the way home, the various distinctions between bulls, what marked a bull as having particular mettle. The fierceness of the Muira bulls. She was glad the Porters were so knowledgeable. Karlo, who had come in her car this time, scarcely spoke, seemed oddly subdued.

It was late when they returned to the house. She was too tired to think of eating, though she badly wanted a glass of wine. She offered one to Karlo. "I am very grateful for all that has been," he said. "Now the ending," he acknowledged, for he and Peter would be leaving the next day for Barcelona, where he would catch his flight.

"You have given me new life," he said, as he took the glass from her hand. "Let me drink to you."

"To your safe return," she said, as they clinked glasses.

He stood looking at her as though he were memorizing her features. "We'll miss you here," she said.

He set down the glass, came and put his arms around her, dived in for a kiss. "I love you," he said.

She did not resist.

"There are many marriages," he said. "I have a wife I love very much. But I love you too—we are together in my soul. Sleep with me."

"I can't," she said, drawing back. "I just can't."

"Oh," he said. "How terrible for me."

The next day he was gone. Just as he was leaving, she discovered his book of Lorca's poems on the table and ran after him with it. "No, no," he said—"for you." She stood with it as the car pulled away. He waved and blew her a kiss.

The day's mail brought a letter from Karlo. She recognized it immediately. An envelope with slanted blue-striped edges and stamps of gray on black, the large printed letters of her name and address. She had to prepare herself to open it, for what always engulfed her in a curious set of emotions. "You entered my space," the first letter said, "and I knew immediately I loved you." What she had done she couldn't imagine. "If you don't love me," she read in the second, "don't answer."

Did she love him? Love. To be so caught up, consumed. Had there been anything that could do some damage? Everything seemed so divided, fragmented. Yet she had written him.

She tore open the envelope: "My darling," she read, and entered the letter like an obstacle course. Not just for the tortuous English that pushed sometimes beyond the syntax into ambiguity, sometimes into sheer nonsense while its intended meaning plummeted toward the outrageous, but the repeated insistence on whatever emotion happened to rule, the underlinings in red ink for emphasis when all was emphasis.

"I think of you always. Your last letter gave me a high pleasure, like always. Your soul is beauty. When I say the name Suzannah, I think it must be the name for love."

Oh, come on, she thought. She should take up painting again, he insisted, be an artist: "I see you as a very particular woman. Creating everlasting fire—that is your task."

If nothing else, his letters connected to what she remembered of his time there, the way the days had reflected him, the way he'd made her see and value her surroundings. Even if she was his fantasy, his invention, perhaps she was drawn toward being seen in a way she hadn't seen herself. She read his letters as though they might lead her to whatever she was searching for.

Maybe he needed his fantasies to get by—his own situation was real enough: "I am writing you from a cafe—bullets are whizzing in the air around us. Who knows what will happen next. The ministry of culture is finally destroyed financially. My job too. You remember how people's savings were stolen—three billion dollars. How cruel! I could have gone to America, my wife and I—but I didn't take the money. It was stolen from others. How could I?"

She began to worry about him.

The artist, especially, works without thinking of death, though it is all around. Maybe he works because there is always death. I think of that moment in the bull ring. I see the bull. I stand looking into the eye of that death rushing toward me. Always I have struggled against the forces that would take from me my life—even more, my light.

Love also pushes the artist to create. He tries to live with love. You haven't lost the sense of beauty. You know how to laugh—to weep. You are so human. I will carry always the image of your face.

It was a letter she read many times. Meanwhile the letters from home were becoming more insistent. When was she going to put the house up for sale? Indeed she had been approached by a friend of Warren's in Madrid, who had made an offer, a generous one. She told him she would consider it, but she was no closer to a decision than when he had first approached her. What was she waiting for?—she couldn't say. Was she all right, her sisters wanted to know. Margot could come and help her with the packing and moving.

In every direction she temporized, putting people off, resisting any decision. She chided herself for her inaction.

Then suddenly his letters stopped coming. A month went by, then another. She asked Peter if she'd heard from Karlo, but he, too, hadn't received any news. He'd tried to call Karlo at home several times, but the telephone was out of service. "I'm really worried about him this time," Peter said. "You never know what can happen. Anybody with a grudge and pistol. I've tried to contact someone I know in the embassy to see if he can find out anything. I may have to go myself."

She resumed her long walks not just on the beach but into the countryside as well. Sometimes she drove out to the villages and walked through the streets, observing old women sitting in doorways, the men in the taverns, the children playing ball in the streets. Although she wasn't doing anything, it seemed that what she was doing was profoundly real. She seemed to live in a solitude in which she wasn't alone. It was more than enough to be struggling with her own shadow.

She was afraid for him. She had an image of him falling between two mirrors, never to be reflected again in her day or night. She'd begun to read the poetry he left behind, tried to imagine how he'd responded to it. She read it in Spanish; then she bought books of other Spanish poets.

She took out his last letter, pushed away her fear for him and wrote a long response she couldn't have written before. What happened in the bullring now struck her as the outward expression of something hidden that she had caught at last. She wrote out a verse from one of the poems she had read:

> You are what I am
> neither more nor less than nothing.
> I dream of a body that bleeds,
> a soul that dreams blood.

A strange poem that sent shivers up her spine—haunted her. She found the words compelling even as she resisted them. Even as she finished writing the letter, she knew she would never see Karlo again. She'd send the letter anyway.

When she went to post it, she found a letter from Margot waiting for her. "We so look forward to the time when you'll be part of the family again," she read. "Do let us know when you're coming. We'll gather everybody together for a royal welcome."

She stared at the sentences, reread them several times before they connected with her understanding. A royal welcome. But somehow she knew she couldn't go back. And if she stayed in Spain.... She didn't know what her experience would be, but it no longer mattered, her not knowing. She would simply let it come to her—come the way the light came. There were moments when she let herself be surprised by light: when she stepped into the patio and let her eye move over the reds and oranges of the bougainvillea as the sun caught it and the red amaryllis, the roses and the geraniums. At that moment they reminded her of blood.

a Garden amid Fires

The lake: a faint sheen. Summoned from the stillness by a chorus of birds. Summoned into light, and form. Then the sun stroking the surface into silk, with a touch of rose—mist rising. Later in the morning a breeze kicking up. The lake, deep blue, surface ruffled, sparkling with diamonds. So she had known it from childhood, with every variation of cloud above it, approaching rain turning all to gray, lake and sky merging into one. Now, so it seemed, it would take the gods to separate sky and water. All had coalesced into gray, with a cry of absence at the heart. "Evan," she wrote, and paused, as though staring into a gap of consciousness. "You are part of this place. Think what we lived here."

It was ground she'd retraced for the past two years, ever since things had broken apart: Evan as part of the family. Evan as father to her teen-aged son. The picnics at Katahdin, the hikes up the trails. Their days here at the very table at which she now sat. It was the gift she'd had to offer him while she emerged from the dark time of her divorce to reclaim the lake, the woods, her garden, taking up the original flow of time and what love could offer: the chance to see things once again in the light of a vital passion.

The sound of hammering interrupted her. One of the cabins, long empty, now claimed new owners. From the other side of the woods separating her place from theirs, she could hear now the pounding of nails, now the whine of a saw. For several weekends and one long space of a week it had been going on. Once when she was down by the dock, a burst of swear words flew in her direction like a shower of stones—ah, open water, that great conveyor and tale bearer. Whoever it was, he had his work cut out for him. When she'd cared about such things, she'd gone 'round to inspect the rotting foundation logs and sagging roof, to deplore the deterioration and neglect. The mice must have been having a field day.

Now there were kids—the first in a number of seasons at that end of the lake—appearing like some endangered species staging a comeback. Two boys, Kevin and Bradley, ten and eight, were already a presence. They kept showing up just under her kitchen window, popping out of the moment, fishing poles over their shoulders. Until August 6, they had license to make whatever depredations they could against the trout in the nearby brook. They spent hours at it. "Hey, Mrs. Lady—" Here they were again. They'd had trout for breakfast, they told her, pausing to give her the latest news of their activities. They intended to catch enough fish for supper. See. They held up their trophies. Kevin had three fish, Bradley two. They were calling it quits for lunch—was it so late already?—but they'd be back.

No doubt. They kept claiming her attention, as though by some previously determined mandate. Kevin, she paused to observe, had sandy, curly hair and freckles; dimples came with a smile meant to be winning, but it was too quick, too nervous for the desired effect—an arrow fallen short of target. A few more seasons and he'd no doubt guess where to look for victories. Bradley, a beautiful boy, she acknowledged—thick dark hair and blue eyes, a spot of pink on the cheek—had a hangdog look. She saw awkwardness and accident, something bred for calamity. He seemed to cling to his brother, as though it were already part of his knowledge.

Since they'd been coming these past several weekends while their parents banged or sawed away, Kevin taking charge,

Bradley struggling to keep up, the two of them had been on the heels of everything that moved in woods and lake: invading the marshes, emerging muddy but triumphant with frogs; snatching up toads and brown garter snakes from the grass; shooting off their BB guns at crows—with little effect—angling for bass at the end of the dock. They'd even set a trap for eels. Maybe they'd go after the bears while they were at it—Claire wouldn't have been surprised. No doubt it was natural, their predatory curiosity, but she saw something almost frenetic in their activity. Hyperactive, she thought—trying to take nature by storm.

Only it better not be her garden. "I see you've got your dog," she said, as the creature, basic black dog, came bounding up. "Remember dogs and flowers don't mix."

"Yes, ma'am." They looked at her gravely. "Come on, Pharaoh, heel."

"He doesn't mind much," Kevin said, grabbing him by the collar. "But we've got a leash."

"Good boy," she said.

It was taking all her effort to rescue a little plot from the grass, it had become so overgrown. In spite of herself, she was appalled at what she'd allowed to happen. The past two summers, she'd done nothing but lie about in a stupor, often not getting out of bed 'til noon, hardly venturing out-of-doors. Fortunately the lilies were hardy—the grass hadn't choked them out—and even the delphiniums and foxglove had managed to bloom.

Now, at least, she clung to the notion of a garden, though not for what it used to mean to her. These days it was so much grass to pull, so many stones to dig out. You could hardly turn your back before weeds invaded every pause. Her labors left her exhausted. But now that she was planning to sell the place, she could go to it with a certain fierce resolve. The garden would be a selling point.

"And so, my dear," she wrote, turning back to her letter, the letter she was always writing—in her head, if not on paper—"have the tigers of wrath proved wiser than the horses of instruction? By all means, put your bets on the tigers. They tore their way to something more pure, more real, oh fire of wrath, than ever horsely instruction could plod to. Love?—toss aside instruction altogether. One dark interlude to blot out the love of eighteen years—how could it have happened?"

She paused, uncertain, as she always did before the loss that had so depleted her. There had been some tough years, it was true, when Evan had had few assignments—something lackluster in his work—and they'd had to depend mostly on her salary. Was that the beginning of his restlessness, a hint of absence, physical distance? Followed by the summer when he'd flung himself uselessly about the camp. Scaring her. She'd hadn't known how to meet him.

"Why don't you do some photos?" she'd said, thinking that some of his best had come from there. The lake. Swamps. The old decaying train station. Portraits of the old-timers still around. He'd won prizes. He'd published a calendar that had made things pretty flush for a while, even taken him to Mexico.

"This place bores me to death."

She'd been too stunned to speak

"You don't move," he accused her. "How can you stand it? You're like a frog stuck in its wadi. Don't you know there's a world out there?"

She had felt condemned at the source of her being.

What was there to say to him? An image came to mind. Still now in July the dark woods were filled with little lights. Fireflies. Off, on. Lovely, but the dark was still dark. Was it that you stopped loving me? Loving who she was, wanting what she was not. She leaned back, her pen having taken her by surprise. Was that why he'd kept picking at her, turning up all her faults for inspection? Stripping her of all dignity. 'Til a tiger, still small, leapt out in spite of her. Surprised him, no doubt. And then it began—the wrath of tigers. Followed by the numbness that even after two years she hadn't been able to dispel, that said she loved him still and hadn't moved beyond that. I hate love, she thought.

"Do you know what we saw?"

Back so soon, or had they ever left?

"No, what?" she said. Who had cast her in the gritty role of patience?

"A moose."

"Two mooses. Only he didn't see the second one. I did," Kevin boasted.

"I did too."

"Okay, boys, trot on home now," she told them, standing up to assume a more commanding position. "Remember, lunch time. Let's take a little break." Dammit, she thought. I don't come up here to baby sit somebody else's kids. The parents ought to know better.

"Hey, there's a car coming," Kevin said.

Her own kid—she'd been expecting him. Daniel, her one and only. She tried to summon the resources for the occasion. For Maria, her granddaughter, now six, was coming as well. A child she hadn't seen at all during the past two years.

"Let's go see," Kevin said.

"Hold on a minute," Claire said. "This is private."

"Hey, it's Dad," one of the boys yelled, as they went romping around to the front. As Claire went outside, her neighbor, a sort of roughened version of his older son, climbed out of his Explorer. As he paused, he gave the impression he had merely stopped to ask for directions.

"I'm John Hurley," he said, approaching. "Your new neighbor." He extended his hand.

"See," Kevin said. "This is the nice lady we told you about."

Nice lady. Claire winced. Had they badgered him into coming over? She worked up a smile. "It's such a relief to have someone in the camp again," she said. "We were afraid it was going to rack and ruin." We—she caught herself. For so many years they had been together. The habit was ingrained. "I've heard you working over there."

"I think we got it just in time."

No youngster, she could see—in his forties at least. She admired his ambition.

"I'm glad I can do a lot of the work myself, though I've had some help. At least the roof's on and there are no more leaks. The furniture was a wreck."

"I'll bet. You've taken on a real job."

"Good for me," he said. "Therapeutic, as they say."

145

She wished they wouldn't. Just let them try to tell her that about her garden.

"But it'll be great," he added, as though to assure himself. "We love it here. This lake, the woods." He gestured with open palms.

"Don't forget the loons," Kevin put in.

"And the train," Bradley said. "And the moose."

"I hope they haven't been bothering you," their father said. "They help me a lot when I can corral them. The rest of the time I've pretty much left them on their own." They had claimed him—standing in front of him, linked together by the arms he had around their shoulders.

Now was the time to state her complaint, but some instinct kept her from it. They were new, she was on her way out. Why create bad feelings? But where was the female member of the clan? Staying home 'til all was put to right? Surely she'd have come up to take its measure, see what was needed. Clearly there was a missing fourth. No wonder all that masculine energy was running loose.

"Okay, boys," the father said, "I've got to go to town for nails."

"Can we eat at McDonald's?"

"Yeah, McDonald's," Bradley chorused. "I'm tired of peanut butter and jelly. McDonald's, McDonald's."

"Come on then," he summoned them. You'll have to come over," he said, as they turned to leave, "when we've got the place fit for company."

She gave them a wave. Oh, don't bother me, she thought.

Her son arrived later that afternoon. Claire went out to meet him as he emerged from his weathered Honda—it was a wonder it still ran—unfolding from the front seat, tall and shaggy. He'd grown a beard since she last saw him.

Claire hugged him and was stirred by a sense of welcome—she was actually glad to see him, though it would be difficult. They would come together once again in reminiscence, once again dipping into their history of shared experience. She looked him over. "The beard looks good, but you're too thin. You look like a starving holy man. You haven't been eating."

"Haven't had time," he said, laughing, as he took out first his guitar, then his luggage. One of the battered cases broke open and various books spilled out on the ground—he was always reading half-a-dozen of them at a time.

"I was hoping you'd bring your guitar," Claire said, as she helped him pick up the books. "But where's Maria? I thought she'd be coming."

"She's in summer camp—Bible camp," he said with a wince. "She wanted desperately to go—a little friend wanted her company. It was dirt cheap, so I could afford it. I expect I'll be hearing a lot about Jesus. That's over in a week. Then I'll go down and get her—bring her back up—if that's all right with you."

"How could it not be?" Two weeks then, if she could manage it.

"I'm giving a recital in August," he told her. "So I've got to practice. I hope that won't shatter your peace and quiet."

"Like having Segovia for a guest."

"That would be far better."

Modesty, she was convinced, was his undoing, along with his passion for perfection. It was in the logic of things he'd take up both some unattainable ideal and the classical guitar—the perfect combination for starving your way through life. Playing for some church or civic group, usually to raise funds for a variety of worthy causes—the sort of gig that yielded him a pittance. He gave lessons to other aspirants for the strenuous life. He was thirty-one. In the domestic sphere he had fared little better. There'd been a brief, tempestuous relationship with a flamenco dancer, a Spanish girl now doing a tour of night clubs in Mexico and Latin America. Their child was living with him now—apparently he had the more settled life.

That afternoon the boys were back under her window. She'd once again picked up her letter while Dan was out for a swim. Half of it she had crossed out.

The two boys had only one small trout between them. But they were undaunted. "Guess what we saw," Kevin said. "A bear."

"Really," she said. In all her years on the lake she'd caught only one brief glimpse of one.

"It was big and it had teeth like this. And it stood up and came running. It was fierce. Roaring." Kevin demonstrated.

"I saw seven deer," Bradley said.

"You did not."

"And a coyote."

"All today?" she asked. "You've been busy." The infantile note struck her, as though they were making their last defenses against a beleaguered childhood.

"Some yesterday," Kevin allowed. "Hey, c'mon," he said to his brother. "We've got frogs to catch if we're going out in the boat." They took off at a trot.

They left the afternoon to settle back into the fullness of light, into the illusion of peace. She looked at what she had written. What was the point? Did she really imagine a letter would unite the broken pieces, ignite the old spark? Years ago Dan and the neighbor's girl, Denise, had dived day after day, bringing up the pieces of a china pitcher long ago thrown into the lake. When they got it all assembled, but for one piece they could never find, and had duly admired it, they threw it all back into the lake. Altogether fitting—like a ceremony, in fact. Broken love affairs deserved a similar ritual. Perhaps she was still looking for the missing piece—as though that would restore everything. What happens to love, she wondered. Where does it go when the vessel breaks?

How many times had she written the letter, crossing things out, changing the wording, recopying it? The same obsessive round. More. It was a punishment. She had locked herself in it—and was angry that she'd done so. She folded the paper inside the recipe book she had out and turned her attention to supper. She had someone to cook for again.

"Smells good," Daniel said when he came in after his swim. He looked around. "This kitchen," he said, as though that summed up the bounty it had offered over the years. "Any hope of a blueberry pie?"

Of course he was expecting one—it had completely slipped her mind. "There's always hope," she said. "But you'll have to help me pick berries. Maybe I can have one when Maria gets here."

"Have you got the canoe out?"

"No," she said. "I was waiting for you." It was a lie—she'd lacked all ambition.

He sat down at the table to watch as she put together corn bread. When she caught him unawares, he looked haggard. She hesitated to ask him anything specific about his present circumstances. There was the recital—good enough. "So how've things been going?" she said. "You like your new spot?"

"I did pretty well early in the summer, and I'm getting a reputation. But it's not like Irish music or blue grass. Something you can do in a pub any weekend." He paused. "I saw Dad."

"Oh," Claire said.

"I hope that doesn't bother you."

She shrugged. She seldom allowed herself to think about him anymore. "I never disliked you father. It's just that work was a dirty word to him."

"Well, I know you went through a lot." It was generous of him. No doubt he'd gone through a few things himself. "It's pretty much the same. He was doing okay as a night watchman, but things got dull, and he invited over some of his friends…"

She sighed. "Same as ever." Everybody loved the man, he was God's gift to conviviality.

He'd probably needed money and given Dan one of his desperate phone calls and Dan had given him what he could ill afford and would never see again. Dan, of course, would never ask her for money—he'd starve first. She'd always had to find ways of slipping him a little extra. That's the way it had always been.

They dropped the subject, and he then asked for news of the lake people he'd known over the years: Who had been up this summer, who'd gotten married among his age-mates, who'd had babies? Nell, she told him, had come through her bout with cancer—that was a relief. The Davises were off to Machu Picchu, would be up later in the summer. Despite distance and absence he'd forgotten nothing of their friends and acquaintances. He spoke of Clyde and Evelyn and Bea and Dolly, as if he'd seen them only last week and brought up anecdotes she'd all but forgotten.

When they'd reached the end of the news and gossip, she primed herself for what had to come.

"You know," she said in a low voice, "I'm putting the place up for sale."

"I was hoping it wouldn't come to that," he said. So he'd preceded her in the thought.

Surprised by grief, tears sprang to her eyes. For love gone awry or for the simple fact of change—that things were no longer what they'd been. "You know how I loved it here. But now. . ."

He stood up and put his arms around her.

"You know, I think about this place—how I was the one who wanted it, who put up a fuss. Mom and Dad had absolutely no interest in it, and of course your uncle hated anything that wasn't the city. If it hadn't been for me, it would have been sold in five minutes."

"I know," he said. "I can't even imagine what my life would have been without being here."

"Only now without Evan—"

"The way he treated you..." She could tell that he was holding in his anger.

"I never tried to hold him here," she wept. "He went off to Mexico that time. I always told him to do what he needed to do."

"I don't think it's that," he said.

"Then what? Somebody younger?"

"He's had to acknowledge he's gone as far as he can go. That's not always easy."

"Perhaps he wanted too much."

"Like everybody."

She had no answer. "Every time I turn around, I'm overcome by memories—they leap out of every corner. Even these dishes, every variety of willow ware imaginable that we've always eaten on. How many hundreds of meals. It's unbearable. And it's all gone—with nothing left."

"Not quite," he countered. "You're here right now making corn bread— If Vermeer were around, he'd paint you standing there, right in that window with the light on your face. Capturing just this moment. You haven't changed."

But it wasn't the right moment: a particular configuration of sky and water, and Evan coming in triumphant with photos he'd taken or the fish he'd caught. And she, light and transparent as air.

"Oh come now," she said. "Don't give me that. Look at me," she insisted. "Can't you see how diminished… I just wonder— Love—" she said with scorn. "Whoever invented it? What a dumb idea—and what does it get you?"

He gave a little ironic laugh. "Experience," he said.

"Well, leave me out of it."

He stood silently, rubbing her shoulder.

"Oh, go on," she said, stepping back and wiping her eyes. "You're just making me angry. No, it's not you. I should be past all the nonsense. Every time I read a newspaper, I think, Wars and plagues and crime and hunger—all this grief and suffering, and me with my little atom. Why is it such a torment?"

"Because you live and breathe—how's that for starters?"

"Yes, well, attachment—what we're all supposed to be rid of. I'll never settle for resignation," she said.

"I never imagined you would."

"Go on," she said. "I've got to shell peas."

"You want help?"

"No," she said. "Just go. It's good for me to do something absolutely mindless." Like digging in the dirt, she thought.

He went off to read until supper was ready, lying on the old couch in the living room with the springs coming through, that they'd somehow never replaced. She turned her attention to supper—the potatoes, the peas, the fish. The steps, the right order. It was supposed to be a relief to tell him she was going to sell the place. And he hadn't reproached her. Only now she was in greater turmoil than ever, as though she were betraying— what? But then what was she supposed to do—hold onto her griefs as though they were a collector's item? The tapestry gets torn and you stare into the gaping hole. Riddle me this: when is nothing better than something?

When she went to call Daniel to supper, she saw he had fallen asleep, arm flopped down beside him, book lying on the floor. She bent down to pick it up, to see what he was pursuing just now, in his perennial desire to know everything. She glanced at the open page. "O wonder!" she read, "A garden amid fires. I have followed love like a camel. My heart is capable of every form."

Bully for him. And who was it—she glanced at the cover—that could boast of such a sentiment? Not of this world. How had he managed to survive in mere flesh and blood? Hanging by a thread, no doubt—like Daniel. The name of the author was unfamiliar to her.

"Supper's ready," she said.

"Oh, I fell asleep," Daniel said, sitting up. "Funny—I was dreaming about how we used to come up here when the Wheatleys' still had the fishing camp. Remember that girl Serene, the one who used to get all the letters from her boyfriends? I had such a crush on her. Always wondered what happened to her."

"She ran off with old McCain, you remember him, the handyman who worked over there."

"Really? When did you learn that? He must have been seventy-five!"

"Lily Wheatley told me. No, come to think of it, a couple of old-timers came around to visit…"

He shook his head. "She was something to look at," he said, "but, of course she never cast an eye in my direction."

The boys were back again the next weekend. They'd been by several times to show their various trophies. Just now, late in the afternoon, she saw them troop by her garden, their dog trailing behind them. They were in serious conversation.

"Aunt Billie said I shouldn't masturbate," Bradley said. "What does that mean?"

"It means when you play with yourself."

"Oh."

So we come to knowledge, she thought. She had been alone for the day. Daniel had gone down to Portland to pick up Maria and would return possibly that night, but more likely the following afternoon. She had put in her time in the garden. The cone flowers were coming along, as well as the coreopsis and pincushion flowers. The lilies were opening. She had gotten out most of the grass and fertilized the plants. It looked good, she had to admit it. Next she turned to the shelves in the living room, still full of the games and kids' books Dan and his friends had grown up with. All this stuff, she thought. Whatever had she been keeping it for? A few of the books and some of the simpler games and puzzles she put aside for Maria. The rest would get the heave-ho. Then as she picked up a couple of puzzles, the sort that have a thousand-and-one pieces, she immediately knew what to do with them. They might even keep the kids out of her hair for a while.

She took the path through the woods to her new neighbors and found the three of them on the porch, the boys bent in concentration over a jammed fishing reel.

"Come in, come in," John Hurley said, clearly pleased to see her.

"I was cleaning out some shelves and thought the boys might like these."

They looked up, eager. "Hey, that's great," Kevin said, taking them, looking over the pictures on the lids. The reel was abandoned. "Come on," he said to his brother. "We can set up the card table."

"Thanks a lot," John Hurley said. "We had been living off card tables, but we just got this for the porch." He indicated the oak table the boys had risen from. And there's a new table in the kitchen too."

"Molly's First Hand Second Hand?"

"You got it—I've been her prime customer this month. New mattresses, divan—the works. Come inside, I'll show you around."

Indeed the place had been transformed. The kitchen-living room was newly panelled with pine; a shine came from the new linoleum on the floor. On the stove, something appetizing was cooking in a Dutch oven. A loaf of bread that looked to be homemade rested on a cutting board. The bedrooms at the back were neatly arranged with beds and bureaus. The boys already had the card table set up and were laying out the pieces. Comfort. Order. Her eye was drawn to a small silver-framed photograph, where a woman stood with John Hurley and the two boys, smiling an odd slanting smile Claire found rather winning, if poignant—her hair apparently ruffled by a strong breeze. It occurred to Claire she had focused on a point of reference, that all she saw had been done with her in mind.

"I remember this camp being awfully dark," Claire said. "I see you've put in a skylight."

"I also took down a couple of trees that blocked out the light. They're stacked up in back for firewood."

"What a lot you've accomplished."

"I took a couple of weeks off just after we bought the camp, and then my brother gave me a hand. Sit down. I've been at it all day, and I could use a breather. Could I interest you in a gin and tonic?"

"I should be getting back," Claire said automatically, then thought, Well, why not. Hell, she could use a drink. "But you've tempted me—" She sat in the chair he offered her. "You have such a fine view here," she said, "right on the water."

"Yes," he said. "You can see the whole lake now. Once I got those branches down, everything opened up."

He had his domain—took pride in what he could do for himself. The roof he'd fixed, the lake he'd brought into view; very likely whatever was cooking in the pot on the stove. Maybe he was using her for practice, to show what he could offer. A wife-price for the missing one. He went back into the kitchen and mixed drinks for both of them.

Before she knew it, they'd talked away the rest of afternoon. While the sun was dropping, and a little wind was kicking up on the lake, they'd been deep into the local history, who had come and gone over the years. He kept asking her questions; one thing led to another, and she had gone through a whole range of incidents and anecdotes, things she'd been repeating for years: the time she and her neighbor, with the help of Dan and friend, had tried to cook a huge snapping turtle in a copper washtub. "Stunk up the whole place," she said. "But the meat was quite tasty." The time the train had derailed, cars with Bunker C oil spilling over the woods, a tank car of gasoline catching fire. How everyone had fled and watched the smoke rising from the shore, certain the whole place would go up in flames. The summer Tim Johnson's Cessna had plunged into the treetops just after it took off—in front of a group of horrified friends gathered to wave him off. Tim and his son somehow emerging from the woods with only a few scratches, the branches having broken the fall.

As the sun dropped and lake was again turning to stillness, it was as though she were handing him the book in which he would begin to fill out his own page.

He considered. "I think being here will do Jenny a world of good. My wife," he added.

"That's her picture inside?"

"Yes," he said. "She's been having a rough time just now." He didn't elaborate.

"I'm sorry," she said.

He shrugged. "One of those things…. But she'll pull out of it." He paused. "I'm sure of it. Here," he said, taking her glass, "Let me get you another."

"I won't be able to make it home." Somehow she was in no hurry to leave.

"The boys and I can carry you," he said, with a laugh. "I've just been enjoying our conversation."

"Dad," Kevin said, coming up. "Can she stay and have supper with us?"

"I was just about to ask."

She looked at her watch, "Good heavens, it's almost seven."

"We'd love to have you," he said. "You'll save us from leftovers—think of it as a golden deed."

"Stay, stay," Bradley pleaded.

They were going to accompany her back to her camp, but she insisted she could find her way alone; she'd been a child here, she reminded them. She'd been in every inch of these woods. She did accept one of their flashlights. But she could have found her way without it. There was moonlight, and the stars were thick. She could see the Big Dipper and the stars in Orion's belt. Her grandfather had taught her the constellations. His telescope was still there in the camp, the satin lining of the case a bit rusty looking. And fireflies flickered through the trees, winked in the grass. Every year it was the same—every July, disappearing in August. Ever since she'd started coming, her grandfather driving down to Bangor to pick her up. Then her first excited view of the lake that had waited for her return. Reflections of the trees in the water, the infinite lights and shades, clouds drifting over, shifting shape.

She slapped at a mosquito on her arm. Another whined at her head. Mosquitoes and black flies—always there too. Frog voices edged the night. For a couple of years, there'd been no sound of them, but now the frogs were back. A loon called across the lake, two short notes and a long haunting one. Answering calls, giggles. Echoes filled the cove. She couldn't imagine the lake without its loons. Or without the deer and moose, even the black flies and mosquitoes. Inexhaustible. Seen by her eyes and the eyes of all the rest. Always the same, and yet always different—in the various strands of sensation and consciousness that held it all together. The widest net was all of it, the source and the thing itself. Generation and demise, gathering and dividing.

A strain of music waltzed around in her head. After their meal of Irish stew and slabs of bread and butter, the kids had gone back to their puzzle, and she and John Hurley had lingered over coffee and sat watching an early moon over the lake.

"I think we need some music," he said, and went to put a tape into the combination radio and tape player on the floor in the kitchen. A moment later she was hearing Glenn Miller's "In the Mood."

"That goes back a way," she said.

"I'm glad the big bands are coming around again," he said. "I always liked this piece." He made a little bow in her direction. "Could I interest you in a little dancing?"

"I haven't danced in years," she said, standing up. It was an odd request in the middle of the woods, but why not. He put his hand on her waist; they joined hands and he led her into the music.

"I just got a tape of the New Swing," he said, "but it sounds very much like the Old Swing to me."

"I was mad about dancing when I was in high school and college."

They dropped all talk and turned their attention to movement and music. He held her lightly, a little pressure signaling the way they would move. It was dark outside now, the lake a lighter dark than the silhouetted trees. It didn't matter that they had to maneuver around the table and chairs. He led her across the threshold into the kitchen and then back out onto the porch. It was easier than she thought, the rhythm of dancing still in her feet. Their eyes caught in the effort of concentration, everything else stripped away but that. A certain fluidity carried them, a tacit intimacy they were unlikely to repeat.

When the piece finished, neither moved to sit down, but waited for the next tune. They glided into, "They Can't Take That Away from Me." He was humming at her ear. Afterward, they hugged one another, breathless and laughing.

"That was wonderful," he said.

Dancing in the middle of the woods. Wonderful! And what was she practicing for, she wondered, having risen to the touches of sensation, the potential attraction that could light up anywhere. It was too late for that now—she had proceeded to the aftermath, gone to the other side of desire. And what sort of territory was that?

She noticed as she passed alongside the garden that the lights were on in the camp. Daniel must have arrived. Maria would be there. She wondered how long they'd been waiting for her. She heard his voice: "Time for bed, Maria. Come in now."

She met him as he was moving in Maria's direction with a flashlight.

"Oh, hello. Where've you been?"

"Just down to the new neighbors. I wasn't expecting you."

He laughed. "We had to come up tonight. Maria absolutely insisted."

"What's she doing?"

"Catching lightning bugs—what else? I think kids can see in the dark like cats."

"How about it, sweetie?" he called. "Grandma's here."

"Hi, Grandma," she heard from down the path. "I just came."

"The mosquitoes are fierce," she said. "I hope she won't get eaten alive."

"I put some spray on her. She slept most of the way up, and I thought I could get her to bed without her waking. Boy, was I wrong. She had to have a jar and go out this very minute."

Claire could see her indistinct form among the trees. A silhouette that could have been hers at that age, two shadows blending one into the other, out in the same woods on the same mission. Green lights in a glowing jar. Could you read by them?

And here she was coming, her face carrying its own light surrounded by dark curls, two teeth missing in front.

"Look, Grandma," she said, running up. "See, I've caught one."